Bug Out! Part 4
Mortars and Motorhomes

Robert Boren

South Bay Press

Copyright © 2014 by Robert Boren.

All rights reserved. No part of this publication may be reproduced, distributed or transmitted in any form or by any means, including photocopying, recording, or other electronic or mechanical methods, without the prior written permission of the publisher, except in the case of brief quotations embodied in critical reviews and certain other noncommercial uses permitted by copyright law.

Author/Publishing South Bay Press

Publisher's Note: This is a work of fiction. Names, characters, places, and incidents are a product of the author's imagination. Locales and public names are sometimes used for atmospheric purposes. Any resemblance to actual people, living or dead, or to businesses, companies, events, institutions, or locales is completely coincidental.

Book Layout ©2017 BookDesignTemplates.com
Cover Design: SelfPubBookCovers.com/RLSather
Bug Out! Part 4– Mortars and Motorhomes/ Robert Boren. – 3rd ed.
ISBN 9781973395478

For Jade

Liberty may be endangered by the abuse of liberty, but also by the abuse of power.

−James Madison

Contents

Previously - in Bug Out Part 3 1

Arizona's Finest 3

Chopper Transport 17

Canada On Fire 31

Willie Pete 45

Civilization in Peril 59

Let's Go To Town 73

Showdown 87

Let's Hit the Saloon 101

Chester Saves the Day 115

A Wedding and a Funeral 131

Capitol Crime 145

Previously - in Bug Out Part 3

Frank and Jane have become part of a tightly knit unit, and that's a good thing, because their group is getting attacked from all sides. The foreign and domestic enemies they've been fighting have teamed up. More foreign fighters flood in from the north, over the long open border between the United States and Canada. The U.S. Army finally takes notice of our friends, and sends two officers and a small force in to help them, but then there's an ambush, and half of that force gets wiped out, as our friends continue to fight for their lives. Officer Simmons, the shadowy man who tried to destroy them before, shows himself. Is he behind the attacks? Or is he actually a on our side, working for the agency? Can he be trusted?

{ 1 }

Arizona's Finest

Frank watched as the man approached, his heart hammering in his chest. *Calm down.*

"How are you nice folks doing? I'm Officer Simmons." He shook hands with Major Hobbs, and then looked over at Frank.

Frank stared back at him. "You remember who I am?"

"You don't forget being shot," Officer Simmons said. He had a smirk on his face. "If I wouldn't have had body armor to deflect your shot, I wouldn't be here now. Why the hell were you packing a .44 mag anyway?"

Frank ignored the question. "So what now?"

"You don't need to worry about me," Officer Simmons said. "I was trying to keep you guys in the Williams campsite because I thought you were part of the militia. I know now that you weren't, and I'm sorry about that."

"We've continued to hear stories about you working against, and then with, the militia," Frank said. "Which is it?"

"Both have been true at different times, Frank."

"You know my name?"

"Of course, we've been watching you and your group for a while now."

"You've had spies in our group?" Frank asked.

"Actually, I got my initial info from Lewis. We captured him after you took out Hank and Ken."

"Where's Lewis now?" asked Frank.

"In custody."

"What do you need from us?" asked Major Hobbs.

"The agency needs to know who the active Islamist fighters are in this area," he said. "We have profiles on many of the Islamists that have come up from the south. We know very little about the group coming down from Canada. I'm here to inspect bodies, if that's possible."

"We noticed one big difference today," Frank said. "In both attacks. There were no militia men with the Islamist fighters. In the several incidents we've had prior to that, they were working together."

"So, it *is* true," Officer Simmons said. "That isn't good. That means that these latest attacks are probably coming from the north. The militia is still active with the southern Islamic forces."

"I'll bet it also means that there's communication between the northern and southern forces," Frank said. "Otherwise, how would they know about us?"

"Yeah, I think you're right about that," Officer Simmons said. "Also not good."

"Do you have any idea why this RV Park is getting all the attention?" asked Frank. "There's a town close by."

"You guys have hurt the southern group, and you've taken supplies," Officer Simmons said. "Their biggest problem is re-supply. Hitting a gun shop in town for hunting weapons doesn't make sense when you guys have a growing number of their AK-47s and a ton of their ammo."

"I agree, but there's more to it," Major Hobbs said. "In town, you have people spread around in houses that can take a fair amount of small arms fire. The Islamists would have to go house to house to take over, and it's likely they would fail. Here things are much easier.

Bug Out! Part 4 – Mortars and Motorhomes

Small arms fire would go through an RV like a hot knife through butter. You only have a few buildings in this park that are defendable at all, and it would be much easier for the enemy to be successful against them than all of those houses in town."

"That doesn't make me feel very secure," Frank said.

"You shouldn't feel secure anywhere around here," Officer Simmons said. "You're in the thick of things at this point."

"So I've heard, from Major Hobbs and Major Darcy," Frank said. "They basically said that we're going to have to step in as citizens and join the fight against the Islamists, since so much of the US Army is tied up in Mexico."

"I would agree with that assessment," Officer Simmons said. "In fact, often the best defense is a good offense. If you go destroy their supplies over and over again, they're going to be in trouble. They can't rely on air drops for re-supply. The Air Force has complete air superiority, and they're taking down any unidentified aircraft in short order."

"Why don't we go take a look at the bodies up front, Officer Simmons," Major Hobbs said. "And then we'll take you to the back. Some of the bodies back there are in bad shape, though. There were about twelve in the back of a truck that we hit dead center with a mortar round. It isn't pretty."

"I'd better spread the word around about Officer Simmons with the rest of the group here," Frank said. "Most of them still think you're the bogie man."

Officer Simmons laughed at that.

"Well, I must admit, I did everything I could to foster that image, and it needs to stay intact outside of this group, so please let them know that as well."

"Got it," Frank said. "Glad you're on our side."

Officer Simmons smiled and nodded, and then he and the Major went out to the front area. Frank went into the clubhouse.

Jane, Jasmine, Chester came over to Frank. Rosie slowly made her way over too.

"What's wrong?" Jane asked. "You look like you've just seen a ghost."

"I was just talking to a CIA agent with Major Hobbs. Guess who it was?"

The group stared at him blankly.

"Officer Simmons."

Jane put her hand to her mouth.

"Oh no," she said. "Did he come for you?"

"It's alright. He's been on our side all along."

"According to him?" asked Chester. "I remember that guy when he first came over to Williams. He was a jerk."

"How long ago was that?" Frank asked.

"Not long before the trouble really got started," Chester said.

"He was placed there by the CIA. They probably had their eye on the Williams Militia after what happened down in Yuma."

"Well, if it's true, that would explain a few things," Chester said. "It bothers me that the police chief in Williams left and committed suicide like he did, though."

"His wife was sick, wasn't she?" asked Jane. "Didn't that explain it?"

"Maybe," Chester said. "Probably. I have a suspicious nature, in case you haven't noticed."

"That true….you won't take me back to your rig," Rosie said, grinning. "You think I take advantage of you."

"I couldn't handle a wild gal like you, Rosie," Chester said. He smiled at her warmly.

"We handle each other," she said.

"Mom! Stop that," Jasmine said. "Behave yourself."

"Wet blanket," she said. She looked over at Chester and smiled at him. "I still try."

Frank just shook his head and grinned.

"Let's pass around the word that Officer Simmons is now a good guy," Frank said. "But he needs to keep his cover, so don't tell any outsiders anything about him."

The group nodded.

"I'll go up and talk to Jeb and Charlie about it, and bring them some fresh water, too," Frank said, and he turned to go. Jane followed him, with Lucy.

"Mind if I tag along?" she asked.

"Of course not." They stopped by the kitchen and filled a couple water bottles. Then they walked the short distance to the store and went up the back stairs. Charlie and Jeb were both sitting at the façade, looking out. They turned when Frank and Jane reached the top of the stairs.

"Hi, guys," Frank said. "Here's some fresh water."

Both of them smiled and nodded.

"Was that who I think it was down there?" asked Charlie.

"Yes, it was Officer Simmons," Frank said. "He's a CIA agent."

"Government spook, huh?" Jeb asked. "I don't trust government spooks."

"Well, he appears to be on our side at this point," Frank said. "I just wanted to let you guys know so you wouldn't shoot him on sight."

"I'll try not to," Jeb said.

"So what's his story?" asked Charlie.

"He's here to look at Islamist bodies from the battles today. I think the agency is trying to figure out if the folks active around here are from the north or from the south, and if they are working together already. He did ask that we not tell any outsiders about him. He wants to retain that shadowy image that he has."

"I had my rifle on him the whole time he was out there talking to you," Charlie said. "I'll be nice, but I'll have an eye on him at all times."

"Same here," Jeb said.

"And same here," Frank said. "Hopefully he is who he says he is."

"How's my Hilda?" Charlie asked.

"Sleeping, last time I checked her," Jane said. "Rosie is a nurse, and she's been taking care of her. The doc is still here, though."

"Good," Charlie said. "I don't know what I'd do if she got killed."

"Softy," Jeb said, chuckling.

"Hey, I was a confirmed bachelor for quite a while," he said. "Sometimes you owe it to yourself to live a little. We do have some history, you know. I might have been married to her. We came close."

"I remember her when we were in High School," Jeb said. "She had all the guys chasing her. Quite a looker, she was. I'm glad she's gonna be ok, all kidding on the side, and I'm glad you two got back together. It's good for both of you."

"Well, Jeb, Rosie is looking for a man, you know," Jane said, smirking.

"She's too old for me," Jeb said. They all cracked up at that.

"She's after Chester right now," Frank said.

"Hell, she'd give old Chester a coronary," Jeb said, laughing. "At least I'd live through it."

"Oh well, I think it's time to go talk to the folks in the back," Frank said. "Anything else you guys need before we leave?"

"No, we're good," Charlie said.

Jeb nodded in agreement.

"We need more cretins to shoot, though," he said, with a sly grin.

"Careful what you wish for," Frank said. He and Jane walked down the stairs, with Lucy behind them.

"What now?" asked Jane.

"I think we should go chat with the Sheriff, and we need to catch Earl, Jackson, and Jerry before they see Simmons."

They walked down to the main road, and could see Major Hobbs and Officer Simmons chatting near the privates who were stacking bodies.

"Looks like they will be busy for a while," Frank said.

"Think you should call the Sheriff to let him know we are coming?"

"Yeah," Frank said. He pulled his phone out of his pocket and dialed.

"Sheriff?"

"Yeah, Frank, what's up?"

"Jane and I are on our way back there," Frank said. We need to chat with you and Earl and Jackson and Jerry. Is Jerry back from tracking yet?"

"Yes, he's up here with me right now. Earl and Jackson are down below."

"Good, be there in a few."

"Alright, Frank."

Frank put the phone back in his pocket.

Jane looked up at Frank as they walked.

"Are you really planning on being in some kind of Citizen's Army?" she asked.

"I don't see that we have any choice," Frank said.

"We've been told these kind of stories a lot of times now, Frank. We need some independent verification."

"You don't trust Major Hobbs?"

"I do trust him, but he's taking off soon. And I don't know how to take Officer Simmons."

"I'm with you there," Frank said. "I wouldn't want to be in a dark alley with that character. He really creeps me out. Those dark eyes. Shifty."

"Charlie and Jeb seem to have a healthy cautious attitude about him," Jane said.

"I know, and that's about what I expect from Jerry and Earl and Jackson."

"How about the Sheriff and the Deputy?"

"I don't know," Frank said. "Hard to read that Sheriff. He comes off as completely out of his depth, and then he surprises you. He is a damn good shot with a long gun, just like Charlie said. He got the drop on those guys when they were running at us from the parking area. Taking several running men out with a big bore bolt action rifle at that distance takes a lot of skill."

"There's the gate," Frank said. They walked through and headed towards the blind.

"Sheriff, here we are," Frank said.

"Good, come on up," he said.

Frank picked up Lucy in one arm, and climbed up the ladder, with Jane behind him.

"How's it going?" asked Jerry.

"Good," Frank said. "Where's the Deputy?"

"He's down with the privates, going through the weapons we captured," the Sheriff said. "It took me a while to calm that boy down. He's not cut out for this line of work, I'm afraid."

"Here comes Earl and Jackson. I told them you were on the way," Jerry said. "Hey guys, come on up. Frank and Jane are here."

"Be right there," Earl said. The trees swayed slightly as the two men started up the ladder."

"Can this thing hold all of us?" asked Jane.

"Sure, not a problem," the Sheriff said.

Earl and Jackson sat down on the bench with the rest.

"What's up?" asked Jackson.

"We got a visit by a CIA agent," Frank said. "He's up front with Major Hobbs now, checking out the bodies of the Islamists up there. Then they'll be coming back here to do the same."

"You could have just called us with that info," Jerry said.

Bug Out! Part 4 – Mortars and Motorhomes

"The CIA agent is somebody we know," Frank said.

"Who?" asked Earl.

"Officer Simmons," Frank said.

"Crap, really?" Jackson asked. "I remember that guy. He's a real Nazi."

"He infiltrated the Williams Militia for the agency," Frank said. "Or so he says, anyway. Major Hobbs got a call from his CO on their radio telling us he was coming, so it seems legit to me."

"Why did he want to look at the bodies of the cretins?" asked Jerry.

"They're trying to figure out if we have the Islamists from the north hitting us, or if it's still the ones that came up from the south," Frank said. "It's a little worrisome that there haven't been militia men with the last couple of groups that attacked us."

"Yeah, I was wondering about that too," the Sheriff said.

"So you want us to play nice with Officer Simmons?" asked Jackson. "I don't like that asshole."

"Well, if he's telling the truth, you might've seen an act, not the real guy," Frank said. "But bottom line, I don't want any of you guys to blow his head off when he shows up over here."

"Yeah, that might get the agency a little mad at us," Jerry said.

"That guy wasn't part of the Williams Militia when we were in it," Earl said. "He was an enemy. Don't know how he managed to 'infiltrate' it, since all of us knew who he was. His story makes me a little nervous."

"Yeah, does he know that Earl and I are here?" asked Jackson.

"I don't know," Frank said. "He didn't mention you, but he knew my name, somehow. He said he got it from Lewis."

"He remembered that you shot him, though, right?" asked Jerry.

"Yes, he mentioned that pretty quickly. Said that he had a vest on, and it deflected the shot. Then he asked me why I was packing a .44 mag."

"If you would have hit his vest with a 9mm or something like that, he probably wouldn't have been injured," Jerry said.

"Should have gone for the head shot," Jackson said.

Jane had been listening to this, and was looking more and more worried.

"Frank, do you really think we can trust this guy? I don't like what I'm hearing."

"Oh, I'm going to watch him like a hawk," Frank said. "We all should. I don't think he's going to be here very long, though. I expect him to be gone after he's checked out the bodies."

"That will give him enough time to thoroughly case the joint," Earl said.

Frank's phone rang. He pulled it out of his pocket.

"Frank?"

"Major, how is it going? Jane and I are in the blind with the Sheriff, Jerry, Earl, and Jackson."

"Good, I figured. Officer Simmons and I will be there shortly. He had to stop at the restroom."

"Have somebody watching him all the time," Frank said.

"I am, Frank. Something about this guy doesn't seem right. As soon as I can get rid of him I'm going to have a long chat with my CO about him."

"Good. See you in a bit, Major."

Frank slipped his phone back into his pocket.

"They are on their way here in a few minutes," Frank said. "The Major is starting to be a little leery of him."

"Did he say why?" asked Earl.

"No, but I'd say let's keep our guard up," Frank said.

"Maybe we should disperse a little bit," the Sheriff said. "If this guy is going to try anything, I'd prefer that we aren't all bunched up in here. It's a death trap."

"You're right, Sheriff," Frank said. "Who stays up here?"

"I will," Jerry said. "Sheriff, I'd switch over to that shotgun."

"Yes, I think that's a good idea," the Sheriff said. Everybody but Jerry climbed down the ladder and spread around. Jerry checked his magazine and cocked his AK-47.

"Jane, go back to the clubhouse," Frank said.

"No," she said, automatically.

"If anything happens, I'll do better if I'm not worried about you," Frank said. He hugged her. "Go. You can leave Lucy here."

"Alright, Frank. You be careful." She went back to the gate and slipped inside the park.

After a few minutes, Lucy looked towards the back of the park and growled quietly.

"Here they come," Jerry said quietly.

Major Hobbs led the way through the gate, with Officer Simmons following, looking warily in all directions.

"Something making you nervous, Simmons?" asked the Major.

"There's been a lot of action back here, that's all," he said.

"How long have you been with the agency?" the Major asked.

"Hmmm, let me think. About nine and a half years," he said.

"Really, you don't know to the day, huh? Most of the agents I've worked with know it like their birthday."

Officer Simmons didn't answer.

"Sheriff, we're coming back," Major Hobbs shouted.

"We see you," the Sheriff said.

"Have your men come out," Officer Simmons said. "I want to talk to them."

"Alright, guys, show yourselves," the Major said.

Frank walked out behind a tree, Lucy by his side. She was still growling just a little bit. Then the Sheriff walked out, holding the shotgun.

"Who's in the blind now?" asked the Major.

"I am, Major," Jerry said. "Jerry."

"Good," he said. "You can hear from there, right?"

"Sure," Jerry said.

Earl and Jackson came out last, and cautiously looked forward.

"You didn't tell me those guys were here," Officer Simmons said. He put his hand down by his side arm.

"They've been with the group a while now," Frank said. "They escaped the Williams Militia."

"I'm going to have to arrest these two and take them with me," Officer Simmons said.

"Oh, no you won't," the Major said.

"You aren't going to stop me," Officer Simmons said. Then he pulled his side arm out of its holster.

"Freeze!" said the Sheriff. "Or I'll cut you in half." He had the 12 gauge pointed right at him.

"Better drop it, Officer Simmons," Jerry said from up in the blind, chuckling. "That vest ain't gonna to protect you from a shotgun blast to the face."

{ 2 }

Chopper Transport

It was a standoff, the men staring at each other with itchy trigger fingers.

"Well, what now, Major?" asked Officer Simmons. "It will be a pleasure to end your career."

Jerry laughed from up in the blind.

"You're no CIA agent, traitor. And now you've got four rifles and a shotgun pointed at you. Please don't drop the gun."

Officer Simmons looked around at all the guns pointed at him. Then he shook his head and threw his pistol to the ground.

"Sheriff, you got your handcuffs on you?" asked Major Hobbs.

"Sure as hell do," he said. "Everybody keep this jerk covered. I'll cuff him and frisk him."

The Sheriff handed the shotgun to his Deputy, who had snuck around behind him in the bushes.

"If he tries anything, blast him," the Sheriff said. He walked over to Officer Simmons, spun him around, and got his hands behind his back, putting the cuffs on. He frisked him, stopping at his left calf, pulling up the pant leg, taking a switchblade that was taped onto his leg. He threw it in the dirt a few feet away. Then he continued on the other leg and stopped, lifting the pant leg and pulling a small auto pistol out.

"Well well well. CIA issue? C'mon, let's walk this guy back to the front," the Major said. "Sheriff, can you come too?"

"Jerry, do you mind holding down the fort up there?" asked the Sheriff.

"Sure, no problem, Sheriff. And nice job, by the way."

"Thanks," he replied. "Alright Major, let's go. I have my squad car up there, and it will hold a prisoner if we need to keep this creep on ice for a little while."

"Excellent," Major Dobbs said. "Private Jones?"

The private came out of the bushes with his weapon in his hand.

"Yes sir," he said.

"Set to get the drop on things, eh? Nice job. Ready to go up the ladder a bit?"

"Yes sir," he said.

"Good, I hereby promote you to Sergeant. Congratulations."

"Thank you, sir," Sergeant Jones said with a wide smile.

"You earned it," the Major said. "Now, I want you to take command of this back section. Work with our civilian partners to secure the area, and also guard against another attack. We aren't out of the woods yet. I'm going up to the front of the park with Officer Simmons here."

"Yes sir," he said.

Sergeant Jones turned, and several of the people there clapped. He nodded.

"Private Bates? Let's talk. Up in the blind, with Jerry," he said. "The rest of you keep your eyes and ears open, and let's keep that mortar ready."

"That's very touching," Officer Simmons said sarcastically.

"Shut up, traitor," Frank said.

"I'll get you, Frankie," he replied. "Nobody shoots me and gets away with it."

Frank cocked his Winchester, and his knuckles whitened around it.

"Stand down, Frank," Major Hobbs said. "This asshole will get his reward soon enough. This is wartime and we still shoot spies."

Frank settled down.

"Earl, Jackson, and Frank, want to go up there with the Sheriff and I?"

They all nodded.

"Alright, traitor, move it," the Sheriff said, and he prodded him forward.

They walked back to the gate, single file, all of them looking around except Officer Simmons, who was looking down at the ground in front of him.

There were more people out and around in the park, now. The terror of the battles was starting to wane, and it was a comfort to most people that the army was there in force.

Frank moved up next to the Major.

"So what now, Major Hobbs?" he asked.

"I'm going to get on the horn with my CO and talk about this," he said, but then he nodded towards Officer Simmons. "We'll talk more when the traitor is out of earshot."

"If you think there's any chance this guy is going to get away, I'm going to shoot him," Frank whispered. "I'm not looking over my shoulder for the rest of my life."

The Major nodded.

They got to the Clubhouse. The Sheriff walked Officer Simmons over to his squad car. He threw him in the back, behind the mesh, and locked it up. Then he came back over and joined the group as they entered the clubhouse. Jane ran over to Frank. She'd been watching them through the window.

"I didn't think he was a good guy," she said. "What did he do?"

"He tried to arrest Earl and Jackson. He pulled his weapon. We wouldn't let him do it. The guy is a traitor, that's pretty obvious."

"I'm going to go out to my radio and have a chat with the CO," Major Hobbs said. "I'll be back in a few minutes."

"Alright. I'm going to run up to the roof and chat with Jeb and Charlie. I want to make sure that they shoot this jerk if he gets loose."

The Major nodded and left the room. Frank went over to the store and up onto the roof.

"Hey, guys," Frank said. Jeb and Charlie turned around.

"Looks like we were right about Officer Simmons," Charlie said.

"Yep," Frank said.

"What did he do?" asked Jeb.

"He tried to arrest Earl and Jackson."

"Figures, those two are traitors to the militia," Charlie said. "I had a feeling he was going to do something like that."

"What's on your mind, Frank?" Jeb asked. "I know you didn't just come up here with a news report."

"I just wanted to make sure that you knew that if Officer Simmons gets away, we need to shoot him on sight."

"Good, hope I get to do the honors," Jeb said. "What's going to happen to him?"

"Don't know, yet. The Major is going to talk with his CO about this."

"Alright," Charlie said. "Good luck with that. I don't really care what the army thinks at this point. That man is a danger to this group, and if the Army won't do what's needed with him, then I will."

Frank nodded.

"Exactly what I wanted to hear," he said. "I'd better get back down there. You guys need anything?"

"I'm good," Jeb said. Charlie nodded in agreement.

"Talk to you soon," Frank said as he left. He got back to the clubhouse just as the Major was walking in. The two walked up to the group, who were gathered at one of the tables.

"The CO was a little surprised, to say the least," Major Hobbs said. "Simmons had pretty air-tight credentials."

"So what now?" asked Earl.

"The CO has some old friends in the agency, so he's going to ask around and see if he can find anybody who's heard of this character," the Major said. "I'm supposed to get back with him in about twenty minutes. Meanwhile, he stays on ice."

"Begging your pardon, Major," Frank said, "but I really don't care what the Army or the CIA says about this guy. We aren't letting him go free."

"No worries, neither am I," the Major said. "We may have to take him into custody at the base, but I expect him to be shot there. We aren't fooling around with enemy spies at this point."

"I don't want him taken to headquarters by people we don't know and trust," Frank said. "This guy is slippery, and we can't trust a lot of people in the military at this point. He'll get away if we aren't really careful."

"I want to know why he risked trying to arrest Earl and Jackson here," Major Hobbs said. "Is there some history that I don't know about?"

"Remember Hank and Lewis and Ken?" asked Jackson.

"Yes, of course," the Major said.

"Earl and I were getting ready to leave the Williams Militia and join this group," Jackson said. "Hank and Lewis caught us before we left, and forced us to agree to be spies."

"I see," the Major said, looking concerned. "And did you ever act in that capacity?"

"No," Jackson said. "We probably would have just disappeared instead of staying with this group, but then the air attacks happened, and there was the incident where Hank and Ken got killed. We decided it was better to stay with this group. We are with them 100%, and we will fight the Williams Militia with them."

"They already have fought with us against the Williams Militia, Major," Frank said. "I trust these guys. *They're with us.*"

"I see," the Major said.

"I still don't understand why Officer Simmons decided to attempt an arrest," Frank said. "He had to know that we wouldn't allow it."

"He probably thought his cover was strong enough to keep me on his side," Major Hobbs said. "I fought with you guys, side by side. Earl saved our bacon more than once today, so there's no way I'm buying what Officer Simmons was up to. Besides, the things he was interested in while we were up in the front made me question why he was here. That's why I called Frank. He hardly even looked at those bodies, but he was real interested in the defenses of this park."

"He was here to case the joint, and if he got lucky enough, to settle scores with Frank, Jackson, and me," Earl said.

"Yeah, I'd have to agree with that," the Major said.

"How are we going to handle him?" asked Jane. "I don't want this guy getting away."

"Is there a jail in town, Sheriff?" the Major asked.

"Yes, there is, but it isn't the best, and my department is really small. I've got two deputies there keeping track of the town, but if some militia fighters were to storm the place, they'd spring him in a second."

"I was afraid of that," the Major said.

"How far away is the base?" Frank asked.

"About two hours," the Major said.

"Why don't you see if the CO will send a chopper?" asked Earl.

"Good idea," the Major said. "In order to trust that, though, I'll have to be sure that the CO understands who this guy is. If he's still thinking that he might be in the agency, even as a double agent, he'll turn him loose."

"We can't have that," Frank said.

"Yes, I know," the Major said. "I'm going to go call the CO again and see if he's found anything out yet." He got up and left the clubhouse.

"I've got a really bad feeling about this," Jackson said.

"Yeah, me too," Jane said. She came over next to Frank and put her arm around his shoulder.

Jasmine walked over.

"Where's Jerry?" she asked.

"He's up in the blind," Frank said. "I need to get him back down here pretty soon, though. And I need Charlie too. We need to get that surveillance system up and running."

"We need some good men to be watching for attacks while our best are busy with that," Jane said. "Wonder if there's any chance that the army folks will stick around until you're done?"

"Worth asking about," Frank said. "This place is a magnet for the bad guys in the area. If I were in charge of the army I'd leave people here."

"There may be quite a few other small groups of people going through the same thing we are," the Sheriff said. "I'm surprised they aren't attacking the town instead of this RV Park."

"We had a good discussion about that earlier," Frank said. "We have a growing number of their weapons and ammo, and they're having problems with re-supply. They know we have their stuff. We are also an easier target."

"Yes, that's true. We have a lot of rednecks in town, spread out all around in houses. A lot of them are cinder block. It would take a pretty overwhelming force to take that town. They'd need heavier weapons than we've seen them with so far."

"Oh, I don't know," Jackson said. "That M-1 Tank was in their arsenal, and they had mortars too. I think this RV Park might have been their stop on the way in to town. Their plan may have been to pick up the supplies, kill everybody here, and then go take the town."

The Sheriff got a worried look on his face.

"You know, you're probably right," he said. "Wonder if they have more heavy weapons? If they do, they'll try it again."

"Maybe the Major can tell us how much stuff they took when they knocked over the bases in New Mexico," Earl said.

The major came back into the clubhouse. He had a smile on his face.

"Good news," he said. "The CO got conformation that Officer Simmons is not part of the CIA. He's a spy, and the agency's been trying to find him for a while now. We have a chopper arriving in any minute to pick him up. There was one in the area doing reconnaissance."

"Excellent," Frank said. "Any chance you guys can stick around here long enough for us to get the security system set up?"

"Yes, I already cleared that," he said. "We'll be around for at least a week. This is where the action is right now. We will try to hide where we are, though. We'll need someplace to stash our vehicles so they can't be seen from the roads or from the air."

"I thought we had air superiority?" Earl asked.

"We do, but they've been flying small drones, according to the CO. He said to shotgun them if we see any. They aren't very sophisticated and they can't fly very high. Basically hobby stuff, but they have cameras and they've given us some trouble in other areas."

"Wonder if we've already had them over us?" asked Frank.

"You'd hear them," the Major said. "They're pretty loud. They sound like a model airplane."

Suddenly the thumping of helicopter blades was approaching.

"Here it comes," the Major said. "Sheriff, let's get ready to transfer the prisoner."

"Right," the Sheriff said. They both went out the door. The rest of the group followed, and got outside just in time to see the chopper put down in the parking lot. Several of the privates ran over and pulled the door open.

The Sheriff opened the door of his car and pulled Officer Simmons out, as the Major held his pistol on him. Jeb and Charlie had their rifles pointed at him from the roof as they hurried him over to the chopper. The privates held the door open as the Sheriff got in and pulled Simmons up. There was an airman inside waiting. He put ankle and wrist bracelets onto Simmons, and then the Sheriff removed the handcuffs and hooked them back onto his belt. He climbed out of the chopper, and the privates shut the door. They all backed off, and the chopper took off and headed southwest.

"Sheriff, could you take me into town to pick up Lieutenant James?"

"Certainly, Major," he said. They walked back to the clubhouse.

"Alright, folks, you saw him leave. Could you help us figure out a way to stash the Humvees?"

"Sure thing, Major," Frank said. "I'll go talk to Charlie. There's a big building behind the workshop that I haven't been in. It looks like a barn. Maybe we could put your vehicles in there."

"Hilda awake now," Rosie said. "You could ask her too."

"Oh, excellent," Frank said.

"Thanks," the Major said. "We won't be gone long. Take care."

The Major and the Sheriff went to the squad car, and drove off.

Rosie and Jane and Frank walked over to where Hilda was laying. She looked a little groggy, but she smiled when she saw them approach.

"Hi, Hilda," Jane said. "How are you feeling?"

"Pretty good, considering," she said. "How's my Charlie?"

"He's beside himself, honey," Jane said. "You've got him hooked real good."

She started to giggle, but then put her hand to her abdomen.

"Hurts to laugh," she said. "Is he in here?"

"No, he's been manning the roof of the store with Jeb, but he's been down here pretty often to check on you."

"Good," she said. "You need something?"

"Yes," Frank said. "The Major is going to stay here with the army for at least a week."

"Oh, thank God," she said.

"They need somewhere to put four Humvees so they can't be seen from the road or from the air. Is there space in that barn behind the maintenance building?"

"The barn," she said. "Yes, but we'll have to move some stuff out of there. We used to run hay rides at the park years ago. There are several wagons sitting in there. The horses are all gone now, of course."

"Is it locked?" Frank asked.

"Yes, it's padlocked. Go into the office in this building. The key ring is in the top middle drawer of the desk. Help yourself."

"Perfect, thanks," Frank said. He got up and went over to the office. He came back out with the keys.

"Earl and Jackson, want to give me a hand?"

"Sure thing," Earl said, and they trotted over to him. They went out the back door of the clubhouse, past the militia vehicles and the maintenance building. The barn stood behind, imposing in size. There was a chain through holes in the big wooden double doors with a large padlock. Frank started trying keys, finding the right one quickly. The padlock opened, but was pretty stiff.

"I don't think this place has been opened for a while," Frank said. "Give me a hand."

He pulled the chain away, and then they grabbed the doors. They creaked as the men pulled them open. There was some fluttering of wings, and a couple of doves flew out of a hole in the roof, over the horse stalls on the far wall. The space was huge, but hot and stuffy.

Bug Out! Part 4 – Mortars and Motorhomes

There were three large wagons, with hay still on the back, and a small carriage in the middle.

"Look," Jackson said. "Swamp coolers. I wonder if they still work?"

"Let's see if the electricity works," Earl said. He saw a light switch and flipped it on. Several hooded lights hanging from the ceiling came on, giving the room a golden glow.

The men looked at each other and smiled. Jackson walked over to the first of the swamp coolers. He turned on the water valve and heard water flow. Then he flipped a switch, and the fan squeaked to life. He looked over at the other men and gave a thumbs up, then went over to each of the other four units and got them fired up.

"Wish we still had a horse or two," Frank said. "These wagons are going to be heavy."

"If we can't handle them, we can just wait until the Major gets back, and then bring one of the Humvees back here to tow them out."

"Good point," Frank said. "What was I thinking?" He laughed.

Jackson walked back over. You could already feel the cold air flowing out of the coolers.

"If you've got the dry heat, these things work great," Jackson said. He looked down at the floor, which was covered with straw. "This is a whale of a fire hazard, though, so we need to be careful. No smoking, for sure. I wouldn't want to pull a car with a hot catalytic converter in here either."

"Do Humvees have catalytic converters?" asked Frank.

"Good question. We need to find out. I think we might want to rake this up and get it out of here."

"Good job for privates," Earl said, grinning. "Let's shut the doors and let the swamp coolers do their job for a while. The Major and the Sheriff will be back any minute."

The men left the barn, closing the doors behind them but leaving it unlocked. They were walking up to the club house when they saw the

{ 25 }

Sheriff's squad car pull up the driveway. The Sheriff, Major Hobbs, and Lieutenant James all got out and made their way to the clubhouse.

"Great to see you again, Lieutenant," Frank said.

"Same here, Frank," he said.

"You guys find a place to stash the Humvees?" asked the Major.

"Sure did, in the barn back behind the maintenance area. We've got swamp coolers running in there now, cooling the place off. We'll need to tow four wagons out of there, though."

"Yeah, and we probably want to rake out the straw on the floor," Jackson said. "I wouldn't want to park a hot vehicle on top of it."

"Excellent," the Major said. He turned to the Lieutenant. "Feel up to getting the men busy back there?"

"Yes sir," the Lieutenant said, and he left.

"I'd better go check with the CO to make sure that the chopper got back to base alright. Be back in a minute."

Jane walked up to Frank.

"How did it look?" she asked.

"It's huge," Frank said. "Looks just about perfect."

"That's great," she said. "We don't have much daylight left."

"Yes, I know."

"Remember that I've got a job for you tonight," she said.

"Been on my mind for most of the day," Frank said. He pulled her close and kissed her forehead.

The Major rushed back in. He had a worried look on his face.

"Uh oh, what?" asked Frank.

"The chopper never made it back," the Major said.

{ 3 }

Canada On Fire

Frank watched the sky.

"How long should it have taken for the chopper to get back to base?" he asked. "It only just left."

"It should have been back within twenty minutes," Major Hobbs said. "Fifteen if they had a tail wind. The base isn't all that far as the crow flies. It's a ways to drive to because of the way the highways are laid out around the hills."

"So it's only about half an hour late at this point?" asked Earl. "Maybe they stopped to help somebody else out."

"Maybe," Major Hobbs said. "They can't get them on the radio, though. That's worrisome."

"Yes, it is," Jane said.

"We should have just shot that creep here," Jackson said. "He has an uncanny way of making it out alive, in case you hadn't noticed."

"Why don't we go about our business and not worry about it right this second," Frank said. "We need to get those cameras up. And I've got some software to write."

"Agreed, Frank," the Major said. "We don't have much daylight left, but if you can get started, and we can get the Humvee's stashed in the barn, it would be good."

"I'm going to go get Charlie," Frank said.

"Frank, I'll go relieve Jerry so he can come back here," the Sheriff said.

"Thanks, Sheriff," Frank said. "Don't you need to be getting back to the town, though?"

"No hurry. I still have the deputies down there, and I was able to touch base with a few key people while we were down there picking up Lieutenant James. It will keep." He left the clubhouse, and Frank did too. He got into the store and climbed the steps to the roof.

"Hi, guys," Frank said. "I have some disturbing news."

"What now?" asked Jeb.

"The chopper that was taking Officer Simmons back to the base is overdue."

"Did it get shot down?" Jeb asked.

"We don't know yet," Frank said. "I figured we should get back to the tasks at hand, though, while we wait for more info."

"Makes sense," Jeb said.

"Charlie, ready to start working the security system?" Frank asked.

"Sure am," he said. "Alright if I take off for a while, Jeb?"

"No problem," Jeb said. "I'm doing fine. Getting a little hungry, though."

"I'll ask somebody to bring something up to you," Frank said. He went down the stairs with Charlie.

"What's the plan?" Charlie asked.

"Back to where we left off," Frank said. "We took pictures of the map we drew up in the clubhouse with the tentative locations for the cameras. Let's break into two groups....you, Earl, and Jackson, and Jerry and I. We'll walk the perimeter and mark spots that will work well for camera placement."

"Sounds good. We've already marked the two spots in the back, before that last battle happened."

"Excellent," Frank said. He saw Jerry walking over from the back of the park, carrying his AK-47.

"Ready to get busy?" Jerry asked. "Don't have much daylight left, but we can at least get most the places marked."

"You must be a mind reader," Charlie said, laughing. He poked his head inside the clubhouse. "Hey, Earl and Jackson, grab those tablets and the markers and come on out. We are going to try to get the perimeter walk done."

Frank walked into the clubhouse, and motioned to Jane.

"Could you get some food together and take it up to Jeb? He's getting hungry."

"Of course," she said. "You are going to get started on the security system stuff?"

"Yes, we should be able to get the perimeter walked and the locations for the cameras marked before dark, if we hurry."

"Alright, good luck," she said. She got on her tiptoes and kissed him.

Charlie and Earl and Jackson walked off to their side of the park. Frank and Jerry went to the other side.

"Got some news for you, Jerry," Frank said.

"Uh oh, I've seen that expression on your face before," he said.

"That chopper that was taking Officer Simmons to the base is overdue, and the base can't raise them on radio."

"Shit, I was afraid something like this would happen. They don't know if it crashed or if the pilot was a plant, I suspect."

"That's about the size of it," Frank said. "Major Hobbs is trying to keep up to date on it."

"He's sticking around for a while, I take it?"

"Yes, for at least a week. We are hiding their Humvees in the barn behind the maintenance shed."

"Good," Jerry said. "I'm impressed with our new Sergeant, by the way. Sharp as a tack, and he knows how to listen too. A rare combination."

"There's our first camera location," Jerry said. "How about that tree right there?"

Frank looked over to where he was pointing.

"Perfect," he said. They approached the tree and Frank pulled out the marker and made a large X.

They continued on to the next spot. It was in back of the buildings.

"There's a good spot," Frank said. "Wish these cameras had panning capability. We won't get great coverage here."

"Maybe we can get some more cameras in town," Jerry said.

"Not a bad idea," Frank said. He went over to the tree they both liked and put the big X on it with the marker.

They continued down that side of the park, and got just past the barn.

"Who goes there?" somebody said.

"It's Frank and Jerry, setting up the security system," Frank said.

Lieutenant James came walking around the corner, smiling.

"Security system, huh?" he asked. "Good idea. Where'd you get the equipment?"

"Hilda's husband bought it a few years ago but never put it in," Frank said. "It will take some work to tie it into the Wi-Fi system we have here, but it's doable. We'll be able to access the cameras from any device on the network once I've got it set up."

"You know something about this sort of thing, I take it?" asked the Lieutenant.

"Yes, both I and Jerry worked on this kind of stuff," Frank said.

"Excellent," he said.

"How's the barn working out?" asked Jerry.

"Well, now that we have all of the straw raked out of here, it's going to be perfect. Thanks for turning on these swamp coolers. It's nicer in here than it is in the clubhouse, believe it or not."

"Good, glad to hear it," Frank said.

"We have a little extra room. I was wondering if you guys wanted us to bring the militia vehicles in here too."

"Good idea," Frank said. "We don't need to have those spotted from the air either."

"From the air?" asked Jerry. "Does the enemy have aircraft again?"

"Forgot, you weren't in on that conversation," Frank said. "The enemy doesn't have the ability to fly anything large. Our Air Force is blowing anything out of the sky that they see in short order. They do have some small drones, though. If you hear a model airplane sound and see one of those commercial drones flying around, shoot it down."

"You know that the radio range on those puppies is short, right?" Jerry said. "If somebody is flying one around here, they'll be within 100-200 yards of it."

"I had a feeling that was the case," Frank replied.

"By the way, I have one of those small drones in my rig, Frank," Jerry said. "I've got a camera on it. Great fun. If we need it for some reason, just let me know."

"Good," the Lieutenant said. "Nice capability to have. We have some at the base, but they're bigger and take trained personnel to handle."

"We better get going, Jerry," Frank said. "We're running out of daylight."

"Alright, let's go to the next location."

"See you guys later," the Lieutenant said. Frank and Jerry nodded and kept going.

"You know what's really going to suck?" asked Jerry.

"What?"

"If that chopper went down in some ravine around here, it might take years to find it. That means we'll be looking over our shoulder for a long time."

"I was thinking the same thing, and I know it's chewing up Jane."

"Yeah, I can imagine."

"Wonder if we'd see smoke if it crashed?" Frank asked.

"Good question. Depends on a lot of things."

"And of course, it might not have crashed."

"Yes, the militia might have that chopper right now. Remember any call numbers on it?"

"No," Frank said. "I'm kicking myself for that now. I'm going have to make myself remember to pull out my phone and take pictures in cases like that."

"Was it a gunship?" asked Jerry.

"No, it was armed, but it wasn't an attack helicopter. No mini-guns or missiles."

"Good," Jerry said.

"Next site," Frank said. There was a good tree in the right position. He looked and Jerry, and saw him nod, so he marked it.

"We'd better hurry, it's getting dark," Jerry said.

"I don't think we'll get them all done tonight. There's about ten to go. We'll have to finish in the morning."

"Agreed. We want a good view of the sites," Jerry said. "One more?"

"Yes, we're almost to the spot."

"So what's the world going to look like in five years, Frank?"

"I don't know, but I've been giving it a lot of thought. Jane and I had planned on a lot of relaxing years, split between traveling in the motor home and hanging out in Redondo Beach. Now I'll feel lucky if we survive the next few months."

"Make plans and the devil laughs. That the next spot?" Jerry asked.

"Yep, that's it. Nice tree right there." Frank marked the spot. "Alright, let's head back to the clubhouse."

Jerry nodded, and they turned back towards the front of the park. They could see Charlie's team heading back too. They met up on the Clubhouse veranda.

"How'd you guys do?" asked Charlie.

Bug Out! Part 4 – Mortars and Motorhomes

"We have eight or nine to finish. Got too dark," Frank said.

"We only have three left," Charlie said. "Catch them in the morning."

"Yeah, it won't take long," Jerry said.

Jasmine saw Jerry walk in, and she ran over and hugged him.

"You done for the day, honey?" she asked.

"Yes, finally," Jerry said. "How are you holding up?"

"I'm fine," she said. "I'll help you guys with the camera setup tomorrow. Maybe we can get it all done if we blitz it."

"Hopefully," he said.

Jane walked over to Frank and leaned against him. He looked at her and smiled.

"I'm going to go be with Hilda," Charlie said. "She got moved into her bedroom. What about Jeb?"

"Somebody will have to relieve him," Frank said. "Maybe we can get the Army to help us out."

"Yeah, maybe," Charlie said. "I'll be back later." He walked out of the clubhouse.

Major Hobbs and Lieutenant James walked in. They were talking to each other in hushed tones.

"Frank and Jerry, have a minute?" asked the Major.

"Sure," Frank said. He walked over and Jerry joined him.

"Any news about the chopper, Major Hobbs?" asked Jerry.

"Nope, it just vanished," he said. "They're sending out some choppers with night vision to see if they pick up any heat profile. This area is huge with a lot of canyons, though, so it's kind of like looking for a needle in a haystack."

"Exactly what we're worried about," Frank said.

"How much chance is there that the crew of that chopper were plants?" asked Jerry.

Major Hobbs looked down for a minute, thinking.

"Of course that thought has crossed our minds," he said. "So far the plants have been lower level folks who joined since the administration started the service for citizenship program. The pilot of that chopper was a twenty year man, so I don't see him being in on it. There were two airmen on that chopper that were recent enlistees, though."

"Could either of them fly a chopper?" asked Jerry.

"I don't know, but I'll try to find out," Lieutenant James said.

"What's on your mind, Major?" asked Frank. "You came over here to talk to us about something."

"Yes, I'd like to have some of my men relieve your folks, in the blind and up on the roof of the store, and perhaps have some of them patrol the perimeter. I need to keep them busy and alert."

"I was hoping you were going to offer," Frank said. "Jerry and I were just talking about it. Jeb and the Sheriff have been at it all day long. They could really use a break."

"Good," he said. "Could you call the Sheriff and let him know?"

"Sure," Frank said. "And I'll walk over to the store and let Jeb know."

"I'll do that," Jerry said. "You call the Sheriff."

"Thanks, Jerry," Frank said.

Major Hobbs looked over at the Lieutenant. "You may proceed," he said.

"Yes sir," the Lieutenant said. He nodded to Frank and Jerry, and left.

Frank pulled his phone out of his pocket and dialed the Sheriff.

"Sheriff?"

"Hi Frank, what's up?"

"The Major is sending some of his men to relive you in the blind."

"Good, I was hoping that was going to happen. Getting tired."

"They are on their way now. We are also going to have a few men patrolling the park perimeter."

"Good. You in the clubhouse?"

"Yes, we're still here," Frank said.

"Alright, I'll see you in a few minutes."

Frank put his phone back in his pocket.

"How's the barn working out?" he asked.

"Perfect, thanks," the Major said. "I saw that the Lieutenant moved those two militia vehicles into there as well."

"Yes, we talked about it when we were back there scoping out camera sites."

"Pretty nice digs in there. Especially those swamp coolers. We'll use it as our command post, if that's alright with you guys."

Chester hobbled quickly into the Clubhouse.

"Hey, guys, turn on the TV. Big problems up in Canada. I was just watching it out in my rig."

Jane walked over to the big screen and turned it on. The channel was already set on CNN. There was a picture of smoking ruins.

"Oh, no, those poor people," Jane said, putting her hands up to her face. Frank rushed over and hugged her.

The commentator started talking.

"Vancouver was hit by a nuclear device about forty-five minutes ago. It appears to have been another pleasure craft attack, inside Vancouver Harbor. This is in the middle of a large population area. We are looking at casualties in the millions. This is second only to the attack in Paris."

"This is part of their attack on us from the north," Major Hobbs said, shaking his head. "That harbor has been bottled up since the nuclear attacks started. This device was sitting there for a long time, waiting. They waited until a perfect time to get Canada and the northern US states focused on something other than their fighters flooding over the border."

An alert came onto the screen, and the video switched to a different city, also in flames.

{ 35 }

"This video is coming from Montreal, Canada. It appears to have been hit with an attack similar to the incident in Vancouver. The center of the blast was the pleasure craft harbor."

"How many devices do these cretins have?" Frank asked, tears running down his face. Jane put her hand on his as they sat glued to the TV.

"Has to be another sleeper," Major Hobbs said. "We were briefed on that harbor too. It's been totally shut down."

Jeb and Jerry walked in and saw everybody sitting in front of the TV screen. Jasmine ran over to Jerry and hugged him. She was crying.

"Oh no, what happened now?" Jerry asked.

"Two more nuclear attacks, both in Canada. Vancouver and Montreal."

"I thought the harbors had been bottled up," Jeb said, putting down his rifle.

"Sleepers," Jerry said. "I was afraid this was going to happen."

The Sheriff and Deputy walked in.

"Oh, shit, what now?" the Sheriff asked.

"Attacks in Canada, Sheriff," the Major said.

"I thought that garbage was over," he said.

"If they hit Montreal, that means they might have more assets in the Great Lakes," Jane said.

"I was just thinking the same thing," the Major said.

"Look, another alert," Frank said, pointing to the screen.

The video switched to Seattle. It wasn't on fire, but you could hear artillery and gunfire.

"The outskirts of Seattle are currently under attack by a large force of Islamist fighters," the commentator said. They are facing stiff resistance from the Army and citizens as well."

"That's just a diversion," the Major said. "They know they can't take Seattle. But they can get a lot of their fighters over the border east of there when we rush in to defend it."

Jane looked at Frank.

"Sarah," she said, tears flowing down her face. "Oh, Frank."

"Hopefully she stayed in Idaho," Frank said. "Why don't you try to get her on the phone?"

Jane picked up her phone and dialed her number. All lines busy.

"We aren't going to be able to get to her right now," Jane said. "Circuits are locked."

Suddenly Frank's phone started ringing. He pulled it out of his pocket. It was Robbie.

"Hi, son," Frank said.

"Are you seeing this?" he asked. He sounded very upset.

"Yes, we are," Frank said. "Are you alright?"

"Yes, we are fine here. LA is slowly getting back to normal, believe it or not. This has become a giant staging area for our military. What about Sarah?"

"Last time we talked to her, she was in Boise with a friend," Frank said. "Your mother just tried to call her. We couldn't get through. Lines were busy."

"Same here, I just tried to call her."

"You want to say hello to mom?" Frank asked.

"In a minute," he said. "I wanted to let you know something."

"What?" Frank asked.

"I just joined the Army. I report in three days," he said. "How do you think mom will take it?"

"Badly, but I'm proud of you, son," Frank said, wiping tears away from his eyes. "Here's your mom. Take care, son. I love you."

"Love you too, dad," he said. Frank handed the phone Jane. She picked it up.

"Robbie? You alright, honey?" she asked.

"Yes, mom, how are you holding up?" he asked.

"Good. What's going on there?"

The phone clicked. Jane looked at it.

{37}

"Frank, the phone says no service," she said.
"Everybody, try your cellphones," Frank said.
"Mine's got no service," Jerry said.
"Mine too," Earl said.
"Yep," Jackson said.
"We are about to get hit again," the Major said, rising to his feet.

{ 4 }

Willie Pete

Frank and the others were in near panic as they looked around.

"Everybody get to your weapons," Frank shouted. "Keep your eyes open."

"I'm going to the barn to get the troops ready," Major Hobbs said. He ran out to the barn, looking in all directions as he went, rushing through the door.

"Heads up, everybody," he shouted. "The cell tower just went dead. We're going to get hit any minute. Get ready."

"We have a patrol out right now," Lieutenant James said. "Better call the Sergeant."

"Yep, doing that now," the Major said. He went into his Humvee and got on the radio.

"Sergeant?" he asked.

"Yes sir."

"Somebody took the cell tower out again. We're about to get hit. Be ready."

"Alright, we'll be ready."

The Major got off the radio, and went running up to the store. Charlie and Jeb had already gotten up there, and were looking out over the façade with their hunting rifles. The two soldiers were up there as well, looking around.

"Watch that road," Major Hobbs said. "We have the dead trucks along the side. If they try to come down there, we'll nail them and they won't be able to turn around."

"Damn straight," Jeb replied.

"I'm going back to the clubhouse," the Major said. He ran back down there. Frank, Jerry, Jackson, and Earl all had their guns ready to go. The Sheriff and the Deputy ran in with their guns, which they had just grabbed from the squad car. Jane and Jasmine and Rosie and Chester were in the back of the room, looking completely terrified.

"The troops are all ready and waiting," Major Hobbs said. "We won't get surprised."

There was the loud sound of a big gun. It shook the ground.

"The tank," Frank said. "Hopefully it was us."

The men ran out to the veranda, and could see fire and smoke rising from the back of the park.

Then there was the pop pop pop from the front of the park, followed by shots from the big bore hunting rifles. Troops ran up from the barn to the front of the park and dived on the ground right behind the front gate. They saw several militia men and several Islamic fighters trying to run away from the fire pouring onto them from the roof of the store. The soldiers opened fire, sending them tumbling to the ground.

"Bring the mortar up there," shouted Major Hobbs. One of the soldiers ran up with it, and was setting it up when he got hit by enemy fire. Then there was a shot from Jeb's hunting rifle, and the enemy fire stopped. Another soldier ran up and got the mortar pointed at the trucks that were attempting to back up on the road. He dropped a mortar round into the barrel and turned away, holding his hands over his helmet. There was a blast, and then the truck exploded a split second later. The soldier adjusted the mortar out a little bit and fired again. Another blast, and an explosion right behind the first truck. That set off secondary explosions that brightly lit the night sky.

Bug Out! Part 4 – Mortars and Motorhomes

"Got them!" shouted Major Hobbs. "Lob a few more back there."

Frank was still on the veranda with Jerry, the Sheriff, Earl, and Jackson.

"Where should we go?" Frank shouted.

"I don't hear anything in the back," Jerry said. "Maybe we'd better go take a look.

They took off towards the back of the park in a trot. Lucy ran up alongside Frank.

"Good, glad our eyes and ears are with us," Jerry said, laughing.

"Let's go kill us some heathens," Jackson shouted as they went.

They got to the gate quickly, opened it, and ran through. They slowed as they got near the blind.

"Sergeant Jones!" Frank shouted.

"He's in the tank," shouted a voice from the blind. "Who goes there?"

"Frank and Jerry and Earl and Jackson and the Sheriff."

"Come on through," the voice said. "It's Private Bates. Jerry, how are 'ya?"

"Good. What happened?"

"The cretins tried to bring a truck into the parking area. We ruined their whole day."

"Good," Jerry said. "Any more back here?"

"Not so far," Private Bates said. "We've got guys checking around back here with their night vision goggles. How'd it go up front?"

"We kinda ruined their day too," Jerry said.

"Jerry?" asked a voice coming out of the woods. It was Sergeant Jones.

"Yeah, I'm here with Frank and the guys," he said.

"Good. We blasted the hell out of two trucks."

"Two?" Frank asked. "We only heard one shot from that big gun."

"Yeah, those guys were stupid. They had the trucks tailgating each other in. We hit the first truck and the blast destroyed the second one as well," Jones grinned.

"Were there any behind those two?" Jerry asked.

"Nope, we already were back there looking for tire tracks. Nada. The trucks weren't full of men, either, so we'd better keep our eyes open."

All of a sudden there was the sound of a small drone approaching.

"Heads up, drone," Jerry shouted.

"Got it," Earl said. He fired his rifle, and the drone blew apart and fell to the ground.

"This ain't over yet," Sergeant Jones said. "Those things have a short radio range. The pilot of that drone is no more than a few hundred yards away."

"Maybe it's time to go grab my drone and fly it over in that direction," Jerry said. "If they see it coming they might even think it's theirs for long enough."

"Long enough for what?" asked Earl.

"Long enough for us to know where to fire the big gun," the Sergeant said. "Go get it, Jerry."

Jerry took off running to his coach.

"You lose anybody?" Frank asked.

"Not yet," the Lieutenant said. "Up front?"

"One private got shot trying to get the mortar set up. Don't know how bad."

"These folks aren't very well equipped," the Lieutenant said.

"And we are?" asked Jackson.

"We have night vision," the Lieutenant said. "It's dark back here. They thought they could sneak trucks back here without us seeing them."

"You saw 'em with the goggles?" asked Earl.

"Naw, we used the FLIR night vision system in that tank. Very high quality picture."

"Well, we did get that tank from them," Jackson said. "That's 'well equiped'"

"Yeah, but they stole it from us," the Lieutenant said. "Those cretins can't even pump their own oil out of the ground. Any high tech stuff they had comes from somebody else."

"Any word on if they have more tanks?" Frank asked. "Did they steal more than one from that base in New Mexico?"

"We don't think they did," the Lieutenant said. "That was a repair depot, not a storage depot. None of the tanks were completely ready to go."

"What's wrong with this one?" asked Frank.

"It was in for track maintenance. It has an alignment problem. Lieutenant James noticed it as soon as he got behind the wheel. They had to nurse it here. Probably took a while....I'm surprised one of our drones didn't see it."

"Oh, great," Jackson said. "So we've got a busted tank?"

"No, we've got a hell of a good artillery piece, with night vision and protection for the gunner."

Earl laughed.

"Damn, Jackson, you are a glass half empty kind of guy." He shook his head.

"The good news is that this thing is full of ammo. It's got a .50 cal on it too. We can move it forward and backwards in this parking lot just fine. As long as we don't need to take it on a road trip, it'll serve us well," the Lieutenant added.

"We know that big gun works, anyway," Frank said.

"And the night vision and the laser range finder too," Private Bates said from the blind.

"You seeing anything out there, Bates?"

"No enemy movement, but here comes Jerry with that drone."

Jerry came running up, out of breath.

"It's ready to go," he panted. He took off his backpack and put it on the ground, and set the drone down next to it. He got the motor going, and pulled the radio controller out of the backpack. It had a small screen on it, which glowed as he switched on the power. He picked up the running drone and stood, then let it go and picked up the controller.

"A little more to the left," Private Bates said. Jerry nodded, and the drone lurched left, and continued on, picking up altitude and speed.

"Private Finch," Sergeant Jones said.

"Yes sir."

"Get that mortar pointed in the direction of that drone, and get ready to take coordinates."

"Yes sir," he said. He ran over and started getting it aimed.

"Pay dirt," Jerry said. "Looks to me like those trucks dropped the troops off. Look."

The Sergeant looked at the screen. There were a couple dozen troops huddled there waiting.

"They are laying low, waiting for us to let our guard down."

"They see the drone," Frank said.

"How far out are you?"

"Almost 80 yards," Jerry said. "Get that mortar ready. They are liable to take off running any second."

"Set it for 80 yards," the Sergeant said.

"What kind of ammo?" asked the Private.

"Huh?" asked the Sergeant. "We have something other than standard mortar rounds?"

"Yeah, there's some Willie Pete here, Sarge. I think it was from that stash we captured earlier today."

"Yeah, give them the Willie Pete," Jerry said "They are out there with no cover. That stuff spreads enough to take them all out."

"Alright, Willie Pete it is," the Sergeant said. "Wouldn't want to be them."

"What's Willie Pete?" asked Frank.

"White Phosphorus."

"Oh, shit," Frank said.

The mortar round was dropped down the tube, and it shot forward. The whole sky lit up as it went off.

"You took out all of them to the left side," Jerry said, watching his screen. "The rest are running almost straight away from us. Make the range about 100 yards and let another one go."

"You heard the man," The Sergeant ordered. The private made a quick adjustment, and then dropped another shell into the tube. Then there was another bright flash.

"Bullseye!" Jerry shouted. "I'm moving the drone up and down the road. It can stay up for another fifteen minutes."

"Does it have night vision?" asked the Sergeant.

"No, but it's got a pretty high def camera that does decent in low light. A few flares back there would help, but if there's anything big back there, I'll probably see it without them."

"Good, I don't want to light things up too much back there, it will take our advantage away," the Sergeant said. "Alright, let's get back there with those goggles and take a look for survivors and more troops."

Six men took off across the creek, heading for the parking area and the road, as Jerry continued flying along the highway.

The Sergeant got a radio call.

"Sergeant Jones?"

"Yes, Major."

"What the hell did you guys light off back there?"

"Willie Pete, sir."

"Where did you get that?"

"It was in with the stuff we captured this morning," he said.

"Wow. Anybody get hit back there?"

"Nope, we're good. Jerry is flying his drone along the highway, looking for more activity. I've also got six men back there poking around with night vision goggles."

"Perfect, good job."

"Anybody get hit up there?"

"Private Pulver," the Major said. "He got hit while trying to get the mortar set up."

"Alive?"

"No."

"Son of a bitch," the Sergeant said. "He was a good man."

"I know. Did you get a close look at the enemy?"

"No sir, not before they got all blown to hell. They sent two trucks into the parking area, but there weren't troops in the back, from what we can tell. It was a diversion. We blasted the trucks with the main gun on the M-1. Jerry found the troops hiding back about 80 yards, waiting. That's what we used the Willie Pete on."

"These folks are just smart enough to get themselves into trouble."

"I don't think they knew that we were here," the Sergeant said. "And by the way, they sent a small drone in here. We shot it down."

"Well, they know we're here now," the Major said. "I'm going to call the CO and see if we can get some night vision choppers out here to find where they're coming from."

"Okay, Major Hobbs. We'll keep an eye on things back here."

"Alright, out," he said.

"I'm bringing the drone back," Jerry said. "I didn't see anybody else back there."

"Alright," Sergeant Jones said. "I wish they would give those things to us. All we have is large drones. They are great when they are flying, but it would have taken us twenty minutes to get the damn thing in the air."

"Still might be a good thing to have, though," Frank said. "I've read about those. They can stay up for several hours at a time, right?"

"Yes sir," the Sergeant said. "They just aren't good for fast tactical work. There were enough troops back there to overrun us. That little drone saved our bacon."

"Well, maybe," Jerry said. "You guys have night vision. You would have picked off a lot of the cretins before they got close."

"Possibly, but there's a lot of cover back here."

The drone appeared and slowly made its way back. Jerry landed it a few feet in front of them.

"Alright if we go back to the front?" asked Frank.

"Yeah, I think we're done now," the Sergeant said. "Thanks, guys."

"I'll go put this drone back on the charger," Jerry said. He threw the controller and some other pieces into the backpack, put it on, and then picked up the drone.

"Don't forget your rifle," Frank said.

"It's in my rig. I couldn't carry all this stuff and that rifle."

"Oh, makes sense," Frank said. "C'mon, Lucy, let's go." She jumped up next to him, tail wagging.

"Maybe we should get some of those drones for the department," the Sheriff said as they walked back. "How much do they cost?"

"This one was about $1400," Jerry said. "I'm not so sure I'm okay with local police using drones, though."

"Seriously," Earl dead panned. "They might see my still with that."

The men all cracked up. Jerry was nearing his coach, and split off from the rest of the group. He rejoined them when they were at the clubhouse veranda. They went in the door. Jane and Jasmine both rushed over and hugged their men.

"I was so worried about you," Jane said.

"I didn't even fire a shot this time. Jerry's drone and the army did all the work."

"Earl shot down their drone," Jerry said.

"Oh yeah, forgot about that," Frank said. "Nice shot, too." Earl looked over at him and smiled.

The Major walked in.

"Nice job, boys," he said warmly.

"Get the CO?" asked Jerry.

"Yes, and he's sending up a couple of Apaches to look around the area with their night vision."

"Excellent. I don't suppose they heard anything about Simmons yet?" asked Frank.

"Not a word," the Major said. "They didn't find any wreckage during their search earlier."

Charlie and Jeb walked in.

"You guys going to leave those trucks in the road?" asked Charlie.

"At least until it gets light. There's no other way in here."

"You won't need the doc to get in here and look at your private?"

"No, he's dead," the Major said.

"Oh, no," Charlie said. "So sorry."

Jane looked at Frank.

"I don't know how much more of this I can take," Jane said. Her eyes were glassy. Frank pulled her close and gave her a hug.

"I know, sweetie," Frank said.

"Why don't you guys go try to get some sleep?" the Major said. "We've got our men on a rotation. They can watch things tonight."

"Yes, Frank, let's go," Jane said.

"Alright." They nodded at the group of people and walked out the door, with Jerry, Jasmine, and Rosie right behind them.

The night air still smelled of gunpowder as Jane and Frank and Lucy made their way to the coach.

"I feel so trapped," Jane said. "It's a nightmare."

"Yes it is, but it will pass," Frank said. "These guys will eventually get tired of losing people trying to attack us."

"How much of our survival is due to blind dumb-ass luck?" she asked.

Frank smiled sheepishly.

"Probably more than I'd like to admit," he said. "But we do know how to fight."

The sound of choppers approached. Frank looked up and saw them. Two Apache attack birds. Jane looked up nervously.

"Now there's a nice sight," Frank said.

"Good guys?" asked Jane.

"Good guys. They're what the Major asked for."

They got to their rig and Frank unlocked the door. Cool air rushed out as he opened it. Mr. Wonderful peeked his head around the corner, and his tail went straight up when he saw them.

"Hi, big boy," Frank said. "I'll bet you're hungry." He bent down and petted him, and the purring got loud enough to hear over the chopper noise.

"Will you feed them, honey?" asked Jane as she headed to the bedroom.

"Sure, no problem," he said. He went to the fridge and got out the cans of food, dished it out into their bowls, and put them down on the floor. They attacked the food quickly.

"Wow, they were hungry," Frank said.

"Good. Get in here," she said. Frank looked over, and she was standing naked next to the bed.

"Oh yeah, I get to do my special job now, don't I," he said, grinning. He walked into the bedroom shut the sliding door, and stripped off his clothes as fast as he could. Then he took her into his arms, caressing and kissing. They were at a fever pitch by the time they got onto the bed, and they ravished each other, falling asleep right where they stopped.

{49}

Frank was awakened by Lucy barking. The morning was bright. He could see that even with the night shades down. He looked over at Jane. She was still sleeping, so he snuck out of bed.

"What's the matter, girl?" he asked her. He looked out the window, towards the front of the park. There were two Humvees moving from the barn to the front gate, with tow bars and chains attached. The army was going to clear the road.

"You two ready for breakfast?" he asked, looking down at Lucy and Mr. Wonderful. "Okay, I guess I can feed you."

He got the food out of the fridge and filled their bowls again. Then he went back into the bedroom. Jane was stretching, her eyes opened. She smiled at him.

"That was nice last night," she said, with an embarrassed grin. "What's the commotion about?"

"They're getting ready to tow the trucks out of the road up there," Frank said.

"They won't need you for a while, will they?" she asked. She pulled the sheet back, showing herself to him.

"Again?" he asked.

She just smiled back at him as he climbed back into bed.

{ 5 }

Civilization in Peril

Jane and Frank walked to the Clubhouse after breakfast. Charlie was already there with Earl and Jackson. They were getting ready to head back out to finish their survey for the security cameras.

"Morning, guys," Frank said. "Seen Jerry yet?"

"Naw, he's a late sleeper like you," Jackson said, grinning.

"Want me to make some coffee in the big pot?" Jane asked.

"Might as well," Charlie said. "Thanks. Hilda would, but she's not quite ready to be up and around yet."

"She's doing better though, I hope," Jane said.

"Yes, she is," Charlie said. "She'll be up and around in a couple of days."

Jane got the coffee pot filled with water and put in the coffee. Then she plugged it in, and soon the big percolator started to sputter. Jane watched the water spurt into the glass cover, getting more color as it progressed.

"Mmmmm, is that coffee I smell?" asked Jasmine, as she walked in with Jerry and Rosie.

"Rather have Mimosa," Rosie said sternly. Then she laughed. "Just kid. Good morning, Jane."

"Good morning to you," Jane said. "Hope you slept well."

"Jerry and Jasmine kept me up at night, with their carrying on," Rosie said. Then she got a big grin on her face and used her thumb to point to Jasmine. She faked a big laugh.

"Mom!" Jasmine said. Jerry cracked up, looking quite pleased with himself.

"You ready to go scope out the rest of those camera locations, Frank?" asked Jerry.

"Sure. Let's go get that done, and then we can come back and have some of this coffee."

Jerry nodded. They grabbed their tablet and the marker and headed out.

Jasmine walked over to Jane, smiling.

"Jerry really had his blood up last night," Jasmine whispered.

"So did Frank, but I was the instigator," Jane said, with an embarrassed smile. "I'm glad."

"Me too," Jasmine said. "I'm so afraid that I'm going to lose him. I feel like I want to hold on tight and not let him go."

"Yes," Jane said. "It's funny, really. We've always had a pretty good marriage, but it was getting a little stale, and we were picking at each other. All of this excitement has us acting like we did when we were newlyweds."

Jasmine nodded in agreement.

"I've got this strong urge to have babies with Jerry," Jasmine said. "How stupid is that?"

"Not stupid at all," Jane said. "Do you two have any kids? I don't remember you talking about them."

"No, not yet, but we were going to start trying. Then everything went nuts."

"Well, you probably don't want to wait too long. Age will catch up to you."

"I'm only thirty five, so I still have a little bit of time. It would be smarter to wait until things settle down, but the urge is strong. With me and with him."

"How come you didn't try earlier?"

"Our careers…..or rather my career," Jasmine said. "I had the better paying job. We would have had to scale some things back. We were saving for it, though."

"And now neither of you are working."

"Yes, that's true," Jasmine said. She giggled. "Funny, huh?"

"Well, that's one advantage to being older. We're both retired now, and our kids are grown. We could just amble around the country for the rest of our lives if we wanted to."

"Do you want to?"

Jane thought for a minute.

"You know, I resisted taking off in the motor home when this all started. I loved using it, and we went out often….we took a trip every couple of months. But I wasn't ready to become a full timer. I liked my sticks and bricks house."

"You are changing your mind now?"

"This lifestyle and all of the danger and excitement has given our relationship a shot in the arm that I didn't expect," Jane said. "I feel like Frank's woman in a way that I haven't for a long time. I like the thought of being cozy with him in a smaller place, with less junk to distract us and more time to focus on each other. Strange how that works."

"Yes it is. I've had the same kind of feelings."

"So just get baby in you," Rosie said, walking up. "You know you want to. I will help with baby. I had six."

"I know, mom. You are probably right. Even if something happens to Jerry. At least I'd have a piece of him left."

"So just forget birth control," Rosie said. "He won't know."

"Mother, I couldn't do that," Jasmine said. "We would have to discuss that."

"Would he be mad?" Rosie asked.

Jasmine got an embarrassed smile on her face.

"No," she said. "He told me he wanted to last night, when.....you know."

"Then settled," Rosie said. "Throw away pills."

Jasmine and Jane looked at each other, and they both giggled.

"Should I?" Jasmine asked, looking at Jane. "Really?"

"Don't drag me into this," Jane said, laughing. "You make your own decision, but remember that it's always a good idea to listen to your mother."

Chester walked in.

"Coffee. I love the smell of coffee," he said. "You girls look like you're scheming. What are you up to?"

"Never mind them," Rosie said. "You come here, you sweet man."

"Mom! Behave," Jasmine said. She tried to sound stern, but she was laughing.

Meanwhile outside, Frank and Jerry were making good progress on their survey. They were almost to the back of the park now, checking out the last camera location.

"There's a good tree there," Jerry said, pointing. Frank walked up to it and made the mark.

"That's it," Frank said. "Let's go back in and get us some coffee."

"Maybe we should stop by the barn on the way and see what's up," Jerry said.

"Alright," Frank said. They started walking in that direction.

"What a pretty morning," Jerry said. "Wish we were just here on vacation."

"I know. If we live through this, I'll be back for some relaxation time."

"What are you and Jane going to do after this calms down?"

Bug Out! Part 4 – Mortars and Motorhomes

"I would actually like to rent out the condo and stay on the road," Frank said. "Not sure that Jane would go for that, though."

"Sounds nice. Wish I could do that."

"I'll bet you've got some years to work, yet," Frank said.

"Well, I'm forty five, so yes. We want to have kids, for one thing."

"Ah yes, that will cost you," Frank said, laughing. "But it's the best thing in the world, trust me."

"You have two, right?"

"Yes, we do. A boy and a girl."

"Thought I heard you say that. They're both okay?"

"My son is in our condo in Redondo Beach," Frank said. "I need to have a chat with Jane, though. He told me last night that he enlisted in the army. He was about to tell Jane when the cell tower went dead."

"How do you feel about that, Frank?"

"Proud but worried. And then there's my daughter. She was living up in Portland."

"That's too close to the action right now."

"I know," Frank said. "She is probably in Boise right now, though. She was on her way here when all of the nukes were going off. After things settled down, we suggested that she stay there."

"Who's she with?"

"Her best friend. They are staying with her friend's cousin. Sounded to me like there might be a little romantic spark there."

"How do you feel about that?"

"At this point, all I care about is that she's with somebody who will protect her. Hope they get the cell tower back up soon."

"I haven't checked since first thing this morning," Jerry said. He pulled out his phone and looked at it. "Crap, still down."

They got to the barn. The Sheriff and his deputy where there, talking to Major Hobbs.

"Good morning," Frank said.

"Good morning, men," Major Hobbs said. The Sheriff and Deputy smiled and nodded.

"Anything on the search last night?" asked Jerry.

"Yes, actually. The Apaches took some small arms fire. There was a pretty large force up to the north, but they were further away than we expected. The Apaches let them have it with everything they had, and then we brought in a gunship."

"AC-130?" Jerry asked.

"Yup."

"That must have ruined their whole day," Frank said.

"Well, we got all of their trucks, from what we can tell. Some escaped on foot. We are sending a platoon up there to engage the folks that are left."

"Were these the Islamists from the north?" Frank asked.

"Yes, definitely, but that brings me back to what we were just talking about before you guys walked up. We have bodies of Islamists and militia men from the battle last night. We think that they were working with Islamists from the north."

"How about that cell tower?" Jerry asked. "Maybe we should put a 24 hour guard on that."

"I did," the Sheriff said. "We found his head in one place and his body someplace else."

"Oh, no," Frank said. "One of your Deputies?"

"No, this was a person from town. Too bad. Good man."

"So what's next?" Frank asked.

"Well, my men are doing clean up and body disposal this morning," the Major said. "If I were you guys I'd finish setting up that security system."

"How long are you guys going to stick around?" Jerry asked.

"Don't know. What they did last night with that gunship might have made things quite a bit safer for you. The big force in the north can't get here easily on foot, and we know we've taken out their vehicles. We have air patrols flying now, and they are noting traffic. If any trucks show up in the area, they had better have a good reason for being there."

"What about the Islamists and militia men from the south?" asked Frank.

"They're still a problem, but that's a much small force, and they are cut off from their supply lines now. They might decide to move south to rejoin a larger force."

"You have somebody hunting them down, I hope."

"Of course, but the militia folks are smarter than the Islamists, and they know this area. They know where to hide."

"I don't get why these idiots think they need to take out the cell tower every time they're going to hit us," Jerry said. "That's tipped us off twice now."

"If they would have known we were here, they might not have tried the attack," Major Hobbs said. "We think the northern Islamists did that both times. They aren't too bright. They probably think you could've called in the Calvary with the cell phones."

"We should find out how many people in camp have walkie talkies," Frank said. "They're a good backup that the enemy can't shut down. We have a set. We bought them to help with backing up the motor home."

"Not a bad idea, but remember that the bad guys can listen in pretty easily," Major Hobbs said.

"I know, but if we at least have one in the blind and one up on the roof of the store, we could communicate in a pinch."

"True," Major Hobbs said. "There is a radio in the tank, but you won't be able to get to it with your commercial walkie talkies. Maybe I can get the CO to give you a radio."

"That would be good," the Sheriff said. "I might be able to pick up the tank radio with the radio in my squad car. We'll have to check that out."

"Actually, you probably can," Major Hobbs said. "I'll get our radio expert to chat with you after we get done here."

"Hey, we still have Officer Simmons's squad car. That might have a working radio in it too," Jerry said.

"Good point," the Sheriff said. "We'll check that out."

"Speaking of Officer Simmons, any word on that missing chopper?" asked Frank.

"No," the Major said. "And that worries me more than anything else at the moment. I'm beginning to think that it didn't crash. I think it landed."

Lieutenant James came running out of the barn.

"Major Hobbs, urgent message coming in," he shouted.

All of the men ran into the barn. Major Hobbs got into his Humvee. He got a grim look on his face, and climbed out slowly. He had tears in his eyes.

"Shit, what happened?" Frank asked.

"Chicago just got hit with several nuclear devices. It came from Lake Michigan."

"Son of a bitch," Jerry said.

"Major Hobbs, isn't that where your family is?" asked the Lieutenant.

He just looked at him dully and nodded yes.

"Were they close to the coast?" asked Jerry.

"They don't live next to the coast, but some of them work fairly close. It's 11:00 am there."

"I'd better get into town and get that cell tower back up," the Sheriff said. "Got any phone experts in your platoon?"

"Nope," the Lieutenant said. "Radio yes, cell phone no."

"I thought you already had somebody that knew how to fix it," Jerry said.

"We did," the Sheriff said. "He was the guy killed last night."

"Shit, he was the guy guarding it, I suspect," Jerry said. "Alright, let's ask around in the park. Maybe there's somebody."

"Lieutenant, here's the keys to Officer Simmons's squad car," the Sheriff said. "I'm going into town with my Deputy to look at that cell tower. Maybe you could see if your radio guy could talk to the tank?"

"Will do," the Lieutenant said, taking the keys. "You be careful out there, Sheriff."

He nodded and walked off with the Deputy.

Frank and Jerry started walking towards the Clubhouse.

"When is this going to end?" Frank said, looking down.

"When we kill them all," Jerry said.

They got to the door. Jane and Jasmine rushed to meet them. The TV was on, showing the devastation.

"Oh, Frank, this one is horrible," Jane said, sobbing against him. Frank held her tight.

Jasmine couldn't say anything…..she just held onto Jerry.

Charlie and Earl and Jackson came walking into the door, chatting happily with each other. They stopped dead in their tracks when they saw the TV screen.

"Where?" asked Earl.

"Chicago in the US. Brussels in Europe. Singapore in Asia. Varanasi in India," Jasmine said.

"Never heard of Varanasi," Charlie said.

"It's the holiest Hindu city in India," Jasmine said.

"They really want to make this a religious war, don't they," Jackson said. "They can't win."

"No, they can't win, but they will do a lot of damage as we destroy them," Jerry said.

"Where the heck are all of the nukes coming from?" Frank asked. "North Korea is a smoking pile of ash now. Somebody else is making them."

"You don't think the bad guys just stockpiled them over time?" Earl asked.

"Maybe, but they're not that easy to hide," Frank said. "Too many people would have to be in the loop to pull it off, and somebody always spills the beans. No, I think they have a second source."

"Major Hobbs has family in Chicago," Jerry said. "He's really shook up."

"I could only imagine," Jane said. "I'm worried about Sarah. I hope they get that cell tower up and running again soon."

"The Sheriff and Deputy just left for town, but we may have a problem," Frank said.

"What's that?" asked Jackson.

"The guy who knows how to fix it was guarding it last night. He's dead."

"Oh, shit," Charlie said.

"I know how to work on those," Jackson said. "I can go into town and help."

"Good, I was hoping somebody here knew about cellular," Jerry said.

"Let's wait until we hear from the Sheriff," Frank said. "Might just be cut wires again, or something simple like that."

"There might also be other experts in town, too," Jasmine said.

"Look, the President is about to speak," Jane said, pointing to the screen. The group gathered around in front of the TV and waited.

The President walked to the podium. He looked like he hadn't gotten any sleep for days.

"My fellow Americans," he said. "By now you all know what happened in Chicago, in Brussels, in Singapore, and in Varanasi, India. Two things are obvious. First, our enemy wants to make this a war between civilization and their twisted view of Islam. Second, there is a second source of nuclear weapons available to them."

Bug Out! Part 4 – Mortars and Motorhomes

He paused as somebody walked up and handed him a piece of paper. He looked at it, his face grim. Then he looked back up.

"We have been able to pinpoint the source of the nuclear weapons. It is Iran. Our intelligence had told us that they were not yet capable of producing weapons, but obviously that was incorrect. In the coming days, we will bottle up Iran, taking out every port, road, and airport. Nothing more will get in and out of that country. We don't know how many more devices have already left that country. We expect more attacks, but will do everything in our power to prevent them."

"Finally, I have a message for Muslims. I know that most of you are good people who don't condone this war. What I'm about to say is painful to me, and will be a shock to many of you. The civilized world will not allow itself to be dragged back to 600 AD. That will never happen. Muslim countries worldwide are now on notice. You are with us or against us. Countries that do not actively, concretely take steps to destroy the radical element in their countries will be attacked by the armed forces of the civilized world. The attacks won't be pinpoint tactical attacks. They will be the kind of attacks visited on the Nazis during world war two, the last time that civilization was in danger of being destroyed. Do not make the mistake of thinking that we will go softly at this because we need your energy resources. We have discovered more of these resources in North America than exist in any other region of the world. We do not need you. We will not rebuild your countries, unless it is clear to us that radical views in your country are no longer prevalent. If you ignore us, we will destroy your country and your society, and walk away. The choice is yours. This has already gone too far. That is all for tonight. Sorry, I won't take any questions."

Everybody in the room was silent for a few minutes, just staring at the TV.

"This isn't going to be over in our lifetime, is it?" Jane asked.

"Probably not," Jerry said. "There are radicals all over the globe, just hiding out. We are going to have to root them out and kill them, and it's going to be a long, bloody job."

"Hey, the cell tower is working again," Jasmine said, holding her phone above her head.

"Good, I'm calling Sarah," Jane said. She pulled out her phone and dialed. Then she put it down.

"All circuits busy," she said. "I'll try Robbie."

Frank put his hand on hers. She looked over at him, worried.

"What?" she asked.

"Before you talk to him, I've got something I need to tell you," Frank said.

"He joined the army, didn't he?" she asked.

"Yes. He was about to tell you when the phones went dead last night."

"I had a feeling that was the case, when you said you were proud of him," Jane said.

"I'm sorry I didn't say anything before. I wanted him to tell you, but I have a feeling the network is going to be bad for the next few days."

Jane hugged Frank.

"You alright?" Frank asked her.

"Yes, I'm the same as you. Proud but worried."

Frank's cellphone started to ring.

"Maybe this is Robbie or Sarah," Frank said. He pulled his phone out of his pocket and looked at it. "It's the Sheriff." He answered.

"Sheriff, thanks for getting it fixed," Frank said.

"Sorry, the Sheriff is a little tied up right now, literally," the voice said.

"Who is this?"

"Your old friend Officer Simmons. You want the Sheriff and his Deputy back?"

Bug Out! Part 4 – Mortars and Motorhomes

{ 6 }

Let's Go To Town

Frank stood with the phone to his ear, his brow furrowed.

"What are you asking for, traitor?" asked Frank. That comment got the attention of Jane and Jerry. They looked at him, and he mouthed 'Officer Simmons'.

"Now Frank, that's not very nice," Officer Simmons said. "Why would you want to make a comment like that when I have your friend tied up?"

"Who's side are you on today, traitor?" Frank asked.

"The same side I'm always on. The right side."

"Yeah, I'll just bet."

"It's unfortunate that you misunderstood my actions at the RV Park, Frank. I wasn't going to lock Earl and Jackson up for long. I just needed to question them about the Williams Militia, but you guys have to go and stop me from doing my job."

Frank covered the phone receiver.

"This guy is out of his mind," Frank whispered. "But he's got the Sheriff."

"You still there, Frank?"

"Yes, I'm here. What are your terms?"

"I just want a meeting. With you, Jerry, and Charlie. And I want to interview Earl and Jackson. You just bring them into town and we'll talk."

"Sounds like a good setup for an ambush to me," Frank said.

"I mean you guys no harm. And I'm sorry for telling you I was going to get you. I was angry. I didn't really mean it."

"Whatever. Where do you want this meeting to happen?"

"At the park in front of the Sheriff's station. In two hours."

"Alright, we'll be there."

Officer Simmons hung up the phone.

"What does he want?" asked Charlie.

"He wants you, me, Jerry, Earl, and Jackson to go meet with him, in a park in front of the Sheriff's station. Is that a good place for an ambush?"

"Yes and no. The park has no cover to speak of, but there are buildings around it. They might have some folks on the roofs."

"You aren't thinking of going in there, are you?" Jane asked. "You know he's going to try to kill or capture you guys. He might have other militia fighters there."

"We can't just let him have the Sheriff," Frank said.

"I'm with you," Jerry said. Jasmine looked at him and started to tear up.

"If you're going, I'm going too," Jasmine said.

"Why?" Jerry asked. "What are you going to do?"

"I can shoot as well as you can," she said. "Try and stop me."

"I'm going too," Jane said.

"No you aren't," Frank said.

"Hold it a second, guys," Charlie said. "I've got an idea. Let's have them show up, but about fifteen minutes after we get there. They can take one of those militia vehicles. Jeb can go with them."

"I don't like it," Frank said.

Bug Out! Part 4 – Mortars and Motorhomes

"I can shoot, you know," Jane said. "If something happens to you, I don't want to be here anyway."

"Okay, if we are going to do this, let's think it through," Jerry said. "We have all of those AK-47s. Those are fairly easy to shoot. I'll get you both checked out on them. It will only take about 10 minutes."

"Rosie, are you alright with this?" asked Frank.

"Jasmine and Jane should go," Rosie said. "Time to fight for family. It right thing."

Jasmine hugged her mom.

"If I younger, I would go too," Rosie said. "You go protect man. Then you come back and make babies."

"C'mon ladies, let's go get your guns," Jerry said.

"I'll go too, and let the Major know what's going on," Frank said.

"I'll go talk to Jeb," said Charlie. Earl and Jackson nodded and followed him out the door.

The two couples got to the barn in a couple of minutes.

"Major Hobbs?" Frank said.

"I'm here, Frank. What's up?" he asked, coming over to the door.

"I just talked to Officer Simmons."

"Oh, really," the Major said. "Where is he?"

"He's in town, and he's taken the Sheriff hostage. He wants to meet with Jerry, Earl, Jackson, Charlie, and me."

"You're going to go, aren't you?" the Major said. "You'll probably be walking into a trap."

"I don't think we have a choice, Major Hobbs."

"How soon?" the Major asked.

"Two hours, in front of the Sheriff's station."

"Good, that's enough time, at least. I'll order up a drone from the CO. We'll take a look at what they have."

"Won't they hear it?" asked Jerry.

"No, these fly high and quiet. They won't see or hear it," the Major said.

"We want to take that militia SUV, and I'm going to get Jane and Jasmine checked out on the AK-47s."

"You're taking your women along?" the Major asked, looking at them. "Not advisable."

"We already had that argument, Major," Jane said defiantly. "If our men are going in there, so are we."

"Alright," the Major said. "I'll go order up that drone. It'll be circling over the town for the next several hours."

"How long will it take to get there?" asked Frank.

"Probably about forty minutes."

"Good, then we'll get an idea of what we're up against before we leave."

"Jerry, why do you want to check the women out on AK-47s? That's a hard rifle to control, and accuracy on those things suck beyond about 75 yards," the Major said.

"It's what we have," Jerry said. "Better than Frank's Winchester," he said, laughing.

"We have extra M-16s. Let's get them checked out on those instead. They weigh a lot less, don't kick, are more reliable, and much more accurate."

"I'm good with that," Jerry said.

"Lieutenant, give the ladies a couple of M-16s and a hundred rounds of ammo each."

"Yes sir," Lieutenant James said. He walked to the back of the barn.

"I'll go call this into the CO," the Major said. He rushed over to his Humvee and got on the radio.

"I've got a bad feeling about this," Frank said. Jerry nodded. The major trotted back.

"Done. The CO is on board, and the drone will be in the air shortly. What's the plan?"

"Here's what we're thinking," Frank said. "Jerry, Charlie, Earl, Jackson, and I go into town in Officer Simmons's squad car. Our secondary team takes the militia SUV about 15 minutes later, and quietly gets to the scene, just in case we need backup. They sneak up to where the meeting is going on."

"Do you want us there as well?" asked the Major.

"No, I think it would be better if you guys stayed here, just in case this is a diversion to get us away from the park."

"Good point," the Major said. "A couple of things. We got the radio in that squad car set up to talk with the tank radio and the radio in my Humvee. That squad car has a loud speaker. When you get out of the car, turn it on. I'll be monitoring what the drone is seeing, and if they make a move to take you, I'll say something."

"Ladies, let's go do a little shooting," the Lieutenant said as he walked up. He was carrying the two M-16s and a box of Ammo. Jane and Jasmine followed him out.

"Have fun, sweetie," Frank said. Jane smiled back at him.

"What's the second thing?" Jerry asked.

"I suspect that chopper is going to show up, so I'm going to have some birds in the air. If they see it, it's not going to be around for long."

"Sounds good," Franks said.

The men turned their heads as they heard the pop pop pop coming from the M-16s. Then Charlie came walking up with Jackson, Earl, and Jeb.

"Good, we get to go kill us some traitors and heathens," Jeb said.

"What the heck are you going to do with that?" asked the Major, looking at the bow that Jeb had hanging on his shoulder.

"I know the town, and I know all the best places to hide out in that square by the Sheriff's office. I'm going to go hunting. And I won't be going in the car with the ladies. I'm sneaking over there now."

"You taking the hunting rifle too?"

"I was going to put it in the back of the SUV, just in case. And I'll have my .45 on me, of course."

"Earl, Jackson, you alright with all of this?" asked Frank.

"Yup," Earl said. "As long as we all agree that Simmons isn't going to live through this."

"Ditto," Jackson said.

"Yes," Major Hobbs said.

More pop pop pop sounds came from the pasture. There was a pause, and then more.

"Sounds like they are getting the hang of it," Jerry said.

"If they have any experience shooting at all, they'll get those down fast," the Major said. "I hope they don't have to fire a shot, though. How come you guys are going along with this? I can tell that you don't want to."

"It scares the hell out of me," Jerry said. "I think Jasmine's mother convinced me more than anything, though. We aren't living in the same world anymore. If we are going to survive, we'll need to do the tough jobs together."

"I'm not happy," Frank said. "But I know Jane. I can tell when she won't budge. Best to just accept it, and do it in a way that will give her the best chance to survive."

"You guys mind if I take off now?" Jeb asked. "I want to scope out some good vantage points."

"Sure, go ahead," Charlie said. "And don't go getting yourself killed, you old reprobate."

Jeb just smiled, and walked out of the barn.

"It makes me feel better that he's going to be in position," Charlie said.

"What's he going to do with that bow and arrow?" asked Major Hobbs.

"He'll take out anybody he sees that is getting ready for an ambush, and nobody will hear it."

"He's that good?" asked the Major?"

"Oh, yeah, he is," Charlie said.

"Are we taking guns?" asked Earl.

"Simmons didn't say we shouldn't, so I'll be packing my Winchester and my sidearm," Frank said.

"Sure you don't want to move over to an M-16 or an AK?" the Major said. "That relic is going to get you into trouble."

"No, I'll stick with this for now," Frank said.

I have another suggestion for you guys," the Major said. "Body armor. We have some. Might keep you alive."

"Now that I'm okay with," Frank said. "Since we will be totally exposed down there."

"Alright, follow me," the Major said. They went to the back of the barn.

Jane and Jasmine walked back into the barn, carrying their M-16s. Lieutenant James followed them.

"Where is everybody?" Jane asked.

"We're back here, Jane," the Major said. "Be out in a minute."

"Wonder what they're up to?" asked Jasmine.

"Don't know," Jane said. "I'm liking this M-16. It's a joy to shoot."

Jasmine nodded, as the men came back out towards the door of the barn.

"What were you guys doing?" asked Jane.

"We just got fitted with body armor," Frank said. "Feels a little stiff."

"You'll get used to it," the Major said.

"I'm glad," Jasmine said. "You guys are going to be out there with no cover at all."

"Yes, that's why they talked us into it," Jerry said. "Maybe you girls ought to be wearing it too?"

"We won't be out in the open," Jane said. "I'd rather be able to move around better."

"I agree with Jane on that," the Major said. "As long as you know not to do anything stupid like run out into the open."

"I just saw Jeb taking off in his jeep," Jasmine said. "He's not going with us?"

"He's going to get there earlier, with his bow and arrow," Charlie said.

"Oh. To take out snipers without making any noise, right?" asked Jane.

"Yup," Charlie said.

Hey, you guys," came a voice from behind them. It was Hilda, on crutches. Chester was walking beside her.

"Hilda, should you be out here?" asked Charlie.

"I heard what you guys are going to do," Hilda said. "I called a couple of people I trust in town. They are seeing some folks there that don't belong."

"Knew it," Charlie said. "They'll be set up for us. Good thing Jeb is going."

"Ah, Jeb is taking his bow over there, isn't he," Hilda said. "Good. They won't know what hit them."

"I'm going to drive you ladies into town," Chester said. You get in the back where they can't see you easily. Then you can jump out quickly if the need arises."

"Good idea," Frank said.

Static came from the radio in the Major's Humvee. He ran over and got in.

The Major came back over.

"The drone is overhead. There's no large group of troops there, but there have been people on and off of the roofs surrounding the park."

"How much time do we have?" asked Jerry.

"About an hour," Frank said, looking at his watch.

Bug Out! Part 4 – Mortars and Motorhomes

"Alright, do we have a map of town?" Jerry asked.

"Use Google Earth," Frank said. "The tablet's in the clubhouse."

"Right," Jerry said. "Let's go back over there."

Meanwhile, Jeb was approaching the town in his jeep. The streets were almost completely free of traffic, but that wasn't unusual for this little town. He parked about a block away from the park, and got out. He walked carefully along the sidewalk, trying to stay under the trees and out of sight. He could see the block right in front of the square. The library building was the tallest building, but it was only two story. *'If I could get up there I could command the area,'* he thought to himself. The surrounding buildings were one story, and they were close enough together for him to be able to take people out with the bow and arrow or the pistol.

He snuck closer to the last street before the park, looking at the back of the library building. Then he heard something. A click. The double doors on the back wall opened, and two men walked out. They both lit cigarettes. They talked to each other in hushed tones, and then one of them walked to the end of the wall and turned right, heading up to the next street that led to the park. The other man stood there finishing his cigarette. He looked up and saw Jeb just as he had the arrow pulled back. Jeb let it go, hitting the man in the heart, bringing him down silently. Jeb smiled, then ran over and pulled the man into the back door. He closed the door behind him, and locked it. Then he pulled the arrow out of the man's chest, and rubbed the blood off on the man's shirt. He snuck over to the stairs, and headed up to the roof. He slowly cracked the roof door open, and peered through the crack. He could see two chairs and a table by the side of the roof overlooking the park, behind the façade. There were two rifles with scopes leaned up there, along with some bottles of water and a walkie talkie. He snuck out on the roof and looked around. Empty. There was a breeze. It hit the sweat on the back of his neck and made him shiver. He crouched and walked up to the front of the building. Then he heard a scratchy voice coming over the radio.

"OK, everybody check in," the voice said. "Sheriff's station."

"Check," said another scratchy voice.

"Clancy's bar."

"Check."

"Library."

Jeb pushed the button.

"Check," he said, his heart pounding.

"Drug Store."

"Check."

Jeb settled down, and looked at his watch. A half hour to go before his friends got there. He watched and waited. The sun was beating down on him. He picked up an unopened bottle of water and took a drink. Then he heard somebody pound on the back door. He leapt from his chair, grabbed his bow and went to the back of the roof. He peered over.

"Hey, Stan, dammit, open the door," said the man below, backing up so he could see the edge of the roof.

Jeb got an arrow ready, and stood up. The man looked up and saw Jeb just as the arrow hit him square in the chest. His hands came up to grip the arrow and he staggered backwards, falling over a hedge and into the front yard of the house behind the library. A woman's face appeared at the window, looking at the dead man on the lawn. She looked up and saw Jeb standing there with the bow and arrow, and gave him a thumbs up sign. Then she closed her curtain. Jeb went back up to the front of the roof and waited.

Back at the RV Park, the men were loading up Officer Simmons's squad car, and testing the radio loud speaker. It worked.

"Alright, guys, it's about 15 minutes before the hour," Frank said. "Time to take off."

Jane and Jasmine ran over to their men and hugged them tightly.

"Don't you dare get yourself killed," Jane said to Frank.

"You either," Frank said. "Sure I can't talk you out of this?"

"No," she said. "But you already knew that."

"Be careful, Jerry," Jasmine said. "I love you."

"Don't worry honey," he said. "I love you too."

Hilda hobbled out of the Clubhouse with Charlie. She gave him a kiss, looking frustrated because the crutches kept her from throwing her arms around him."

The men all squeezed into the squad car. Major Hobbs came running over.

"Jeb is on the roof of the library now. He has a commanding view of the other buildings. He took out both sentries that were manning that building. I don't think Simmons has any idea."

"That's Jeb," Charlie said, chuckling. "They aren't going to know what hit them."

"Let's go," Frank said. He got into the back next to Jerry, and Charlie got into the driver's seat. They drove out of the park.

Jane and Jasmine looked at each other, and then at Hilda. All of them were on the verge of tears.

"We can do this," Jasmine said.

"I'm not afraid," Jane said. "I'm pissed. This asshole isn't going to win."

Chester walked out.

"You gals ready to load up?" he asked.

"Yes, let's go," Jane said. The three of them walked back to the barn, and got into the militia SUV. Chester fired it up and backed it out of the barn. As he was about to drive off, the Lieutenant came running up. He had a box in both hands.

"Chester, do you remember how to use these?" He passed the box into the window. It was heavy.

"Hand grenades," he said, cracking up. "Yeah, threw more than one of these in Korea. These might come in handy."

{ 75 }

"Good," the Lieutenant said. "Good luck to all of you."

Chester nodded and drove off towards the gate. Hilda watched them. She stayed in the driveway, looking past the gate, for long after they were out of sight.

{ 7 }

Showdown

Charlie drove down the main road into town. As they got closer, the sparse buildings thickened, mostly rundown buildings from the mid-50s and early 60s. Then there was downtown. It was dense, and had a 1930s look to it. The streets were deserted.

"The Sheriff's station is right around the corner," Charlie said. "I'll park in front, and we can walk across the street."

"Why there?" Jerry said.

"Well, for one thing, it will be harder for the snipers on the roof to hit it without showing themselves," Charlie said. He laughed, but it was a nervous laugh.

They rounded the corner, and could see the edge of the park. Charlie slowed down, looking in all directions.

"Is that the Sheriff?" asked Jerry, pointing.

The Sheriff, his shirt torn and bloodied, was chained onto the swing set at the park, and his arms were stretched out like wings. His head hung down.

"Is he alive?" asked Earl.

"He'd better be," Charlie said. He pulled the car in front of the Sheriff's station. It was shaded by the buildings. The men got out cautiously and picked up their weapons, cocking them, and taking off the safeties. They walked slowly across the street, looking in all directions. Nobody was around yet. They approached the Sheriff. The men could see him breathing.

"Sheriff," Frank said in a loud whisper. His head jerked up, and he saw them.

"It's a trap," he croaked. Frank rushed over to him, pulling a water bottle out of his pocket. He lifted the Sheriff's head and poured water into his mouth, as the other men covered him, looking up at the buildings and towards the back end of the park.

"Gentleman," a loud voice said, coming from behind them. They saw Officer Simmons walking out of the Sheriff's station.

"Where's the Deputy?" asked Charlie.

"Sorry, he didn't make it," Officer Simmons said, with a fake look of sorrow on his face. "I'd appreciate it if you would put those guns down."

"Yeah, I'll just bet you would, asshole," Jackson said. He pointed his rifle right at Officer Simmons's head.

"We've got you guys covered from all sides," Officer Simmons said mildly. "Put them down."

"Stuff it," Earl said.

Frank glanced up on the Library. Jeb was up there. He did a quick salute, and then got back out of sight. Frank repressed the urge to grin.

"Here, I'll take off my sidearm," Officer Simmons said. He unbuckled his gun belt and dropped it at his feet, and continued on across the street.

Frank looked at his friends. He nodded at them, and moved his eyes up to the library. He cracked a slight grin, and then set down his Winchester at his feet. The other men set their guns down at their feet as well, and turned to watch Officer Simmons as he approached.

"There, that wasn't so hard, was it?" Simmons asked.

"What kind of deal do you want?" Jerry asked.

"I just want to talk to Earl and Jackson, like I said. You let me do that, and I'll let all of you fine people walk right out of here."

Bug Out! Part 4 – Mortars and Motorhomes

"Alright, talk," Frank said.

"Not *here*," Officer Simmons said. "In the jail."

"No, we aren't letting Earl and Jackson out of our sight, traitor," Jerry said. "Talk to them right here."

"That's really not nice, Jerry," Officer Simmons said. "You shouldn't treat me like that. I just might take that out on your pretty wife."

Jerry lurched for his gun, and a shot came from the roof to the right of the library, hitting the ground about six inches from the AK-47. Jerry froze. Frank glanced up just in time to see Jeb stand up and let an arrow go. He looked down at Frank and gave a thumbs up, then sank out of sight again.

"Why, Jerry, are you upset with me?" asked Officer Simmons. "I was only kidding. You know, like Frank was when he shot me with that .44 mag relic."

Frank glared at him.

"Alright, tell us what you really want, Simmons," Frank said. "I'm getting tired of this crap. I've got things to do."

"Yes, and people to see, too, I suspect," Officer Simmons said, chuckling. "You guys aren't going anywhere."

"On whose authority are you going to hold us?" asked Jackson.

"Mine."

Jackson laughed out loud.

"You? You're just a garden variety nutcase, Simmons. You try to hold on to me and I'll take you apart."

"You'll regret that comment, hillbilly." Officer Simmons raised his hand. A man stood up on the roof to the left of the library. He fired his rifle, and a bullet tore into the Sheriff's left upper arm, causing him to cry out in pain.

"You piece of shit," Jerry said. He looked up at Simmons, and out of the corner of his eye he saw Jeb stand up and let an arrow go. The man on the roof with the rifle fell over. The rifle fell out of his hand, falling to the sidewalk and making a loud crash. Officer Simmons whirled around, trying to see what happened. Jerry cracked up.

"Something wrong, nutcase?" he asked.

Officer Simmons turned back around, then went for something behind his back. He pulled out a small pistol and pointed it at Jerry. Earl saw that, and lurched forward, tackling Officer Simmons. The gun flew out of his hand. Charlie dived for it, covering it with his body. Another shot came from the roof, hitting Earl in the calf. He rolled off of Officer Simmons, holding his leg. Simmons grabbed the pistol from Charlie and turned to Jerry, who was almost to his rifle. He aimed, and then a woman's voice yelled out.

"Freeze!"

It was Jasmine. She was standing next to the battered SUV, her M-16 pointed at Officer Simmons. He stopped, but then put his hand in the air again. Nothing happened. He shook his hand impatiently. Still nothing.

"Uh, something wrong, scumbag?" asked Frank.

Simmons slowly turned towards the buildings. Jeb was standing there, bow in hand. He had a big grin on his face.

Officer Simmons screamed with rage, then turned around and shot Jerry square in the chest. Jerry clutched his chest and rolled on the ground.

Jasmine screamed "Nooooooooo!" and fired, hitting Officer Simmons in the side and in the shoulder. He fell, but then got back up and pointed his gun towards Frank. He fired, hitting Frank in the chest. Then his head exploded. The men looked back and saw Jane, gun still aimed at where Officer's Simmons head was, as he slumped to the ground.

Jasmine and Jane ran over and dived down next to their men. Jerry turned over to Jasmine and smiled.

Bug Out! Part 4 – Mortars and Motorhomes

"Jerry, how badly are you hurt?" she cried. There was no blood. She clawed at his shirt, pulling it out of the way. There was a bullet stuck in the body armor.

"I'm going to have a big bruise," Jerry said. He pulled Jasmine to him and kissed her. "Glad we let you girls show up."

Frank got up and Jane was next to him, pulling his shirt out of the way.

"Damn, these things work really well against a small pistol," he said.

Jane threw herself at him, hugging him and kissing him.

Chester hobbled across the street towards the group.

"Get down!" Jeb shouted from the roof. Everybody hit the dirt, and Jeb fired the hunting rifle three times. They all turned and saw one man on the ground and two more staggering forward in agony. Jeb fired again, sending one of the men flying backwards. The other man shuddered and fell.

Then there was silence. Everybody looked around nervously, waiting for another attack.

"I think that's it," Jeb shouted from the roof. "Don't see any other movement."

"I'll get the Doc out here," Charlie said. "Earl, you with us?"

"I'll be alright, Charlie. It's a flesh wound. Missed the bone, thank God. I'm more worried about the Sheriff."

"Sheriff, can you hear me?" cried Charlie. He lifted his head slowly. He was in pain, but he smiled. Then his smile turned, and he started to cry.

"That bastard shot my nephew," he croaked between sobs.

"Where is he?" asked Charlie.

"In the jail," the Sheriff said.

"Anybody else in there?" he asked.

"Some creep named Lewis, but he took off this morning, with about ten men. They headed south on the highway."

Chester walked over to the Sheriff and put his hand on his uninjured shoulder.

"Glad you made it out of this alive, old friend," Chester said.

"Wonder if they were going back to the RV Park?" asked Jackson. "They'll get a big surprise if they do."

"We would have heard the gunfire from here, I suspect," Charlie said. "Doc is on the way, and the paramedics will be here in a few seconds. They're over at the firehouse…that's only a block or two away."

Just as he said that, the paramedic vehicle came into view. It drove right onto the park next to them. The two men leaped out.

"Who's hurt?" asked one of them.

"Earl," Charlie said, pointing. "And the Sheriff, of course. There's somebody shot in the Sheriff's station, too. Probably dead, but we aren't sure."

"Let's see if Officer Simmons had the key to those padlocks in his pocket," Jerry said, looking over at the chains that were holding the Sheriff up. He went over to his body and started going through his pockets. He brought out a key chain and a loose key.

"That looks like a padlock key to me," Jackson said. "I'll give you a hand."

The two men walked over to the Sheriff, joined by the paramedics. Jerry tried the key. The first padlock opened, and the men steadied the sheriff. The key worked in the second padlock too. The men slowly lowered the Sheriff to the ground.

"Better get a tourniquet on the Sheriff's arm," Chester said. "Lot of blood coming out."

"Who wants to go into the Sheriff's station with me?" asked Jerry.

"Me," Jasmine said. Jackson nodded too, and they walked across the street. Jerry pulled the door open slowly and peered in. There was blood on the floor. Somebody moaned.

"Sounds like somebody is alive in here," Jerry said. They all rushed in.

The deputy was lying in a pool of blood. It appeared that he was shot in the stomach. He moaned again.

"I'll tell the paramedics," Jackson said. He ran out the door. The doctor was just pulling up, and he motioned him over. The doctor rushed into the jail. He looked the Deputy over. He had a grim look on his face.

"He's bad," said the Doctor. "We need to get him to the hospital now."

The paramedics moved the ambulance in front of the Sheriff's station and came running. They got the deputy on a gurney and loaded him quickly into the back of their ambulance. Then they took off, siren wailing.

"Who else is hurt?" asked the Doctor.

"The Sheriff is hurt pretty bad," Jerry said. "He's out on the playground across the street. Earl was shot too, in the thigh. Looks like a flesh wound, though."

The doctor left the station house and trotted across the street. He saw Earl sitting up. His thigh had been bandaged, and he was smiling.

"Hi, Doc," he said. "I'm okay, but the Sheriff's in bad shape."

The Doctor kneeled by the Sheriff.

"Sheriff, can you hear me?" he said in a loud voice. The Sheriff nodded, his eyes barely opened. There was a tourniquet on his upper arm and a bandage below.

"This wound probably isn't going to kill him, but he's been out in the sun too long without water.

"I gave him some water about ten minutes ago," Frank said.

"He needs to get to the hospital too," the Doctor said. He pulled out his cellphone and dialed.

After his call, he put his cellphone back in his pocket, and looked at Earl.

"I'm going to take you to the hospital as well," the Doctor said. "We don't want to risk an infection. I want to take a good look at your wound."

"No problem, Doc," Earl said.

Jerry and Jasmine came running back over. They got close to Frank and Jane and whispered.

"There are two other deputies in the station," Jerry whispered. "Both dead. Somebody hanged them inside the jail cell."

"Oh, no," Jane said. "That animal."

"Anybody else in the jail?" asked Frank.

"Not that we could see," Jasmine said. "The place was ransacked, though. They were looking for something."

"I know what they were looking for," Jerry said. "There were gun registration papers all over the table. After they were done with us, they were going to go around and collect weapons, I suspect."

"They might have tried," Jeb said, walking over to them. "I know a lot of people here. No way would they be handing over their guns to a police officer from Arizona. They would have blown him away."

"Nice shooting up there, Jeb," Frank said. "You saved our butts again."

Jeb nodded and smiled.

"You might want to radio the Major and let him know about Lewis," Jerry said.

"Yeah, you're right," Frank said. He trotted over to the squad car and got into the driver's seat.

"A couple of you guys want to help me get the bodies off the roof?" Jeb asked. Charlie and Jackson and Jerry nodded, and they took off towards the buildings.

Frank picked up the microphone on the radio as Jane walked over.

"Major Hobbs? Come in."

There was a few seconds of silence. Then a click.

"Hobbs here. Frank?"

"Yep. Anything going on there?"

"No, it's been quiet. We heard the gunfire from town. Everybody alright?"

"Earl got hit, but not bad. The Sheriff is in bad shape, and so is the Deputy. The Deputy is on the way to the hospital now, and then they'll be picking up the Sheriff."

"How about Simmons?"

"Jasmine and Jane took care of that creep. Jeb took out his snipers up on the roofs with his bow and arrow. We might have a problem, though."

"What's that?"

"Lewis is out. He was here in the morning. He took off towards the south with about ten men before we got here."

"Who told you that?"

"The Sheriff. Obviously they aren't planning to hit the RV Park, at least for now, or you would have seen them already."

"Do you know what they were driving, Frank? The drone is still in the air."

"I'll ask the Sheriff and get back to you."

"Okay, talk to you soon. Out."

Frank got out of the squad car and shut the door. Jane hugged him.

"You okay?" Frank asked. "Does it bother you killing Simmons?"

"That doesn't bother me a bit," Jane said. "That creep didn't deserve to live. It bothers me what they did to the Sheriff. And I keep seeing you getting shot again and again in my mind."

"I'm sorry I tried to stop you from coming," Frank said.

"Don't worry about that, Frank," she said. "I understand. It's alright."

"Let's go see if the Sheriff can tell us what Lewis was driving," Frank said. They went back across the street to the Sheriff. The doc was kneeling by him, trying to make him comfortable.

"Sheriff, can you talk?" Frank asked. His eyes opened up slightly, and his head turned towards Frank.

"Not too much, Frank. He's pretty weak," the Doc said.

"Just one question," Frank said. "Did you see what Lewis and his men were driving when they left?"

The Sheriff nodded yes, and smiled.

"Class C," he croaked.

"Motorhome?" Frank asked.

The Sheriff nodded.

"Perfect, thanks, Sheriff. I'm going to go radio the Major….the drone is still in the air. Maybe they can find him."

The Sheriff smiled at Frank and nodded.

Frank trotted back across the street to the squad car and got on the radio.

"Major Hobbs?"

"I'm here Frank. What did you find out?"

"Lewis and his men left in a Class C motorhome."

"Class C – that's the kind with the cab in the front, right?"

"Yep."

"Well, I doubt if there are many of those out and about. I'll get the drone headed down south, and see if the CO will put some choppers in the air to look as well. Thanks Frank."

"Welcome, Major. Watch the front gate. They might try to use that motorhome as a Trojan horse."

"We'll watch for it. Out."

Jeb and Charlie and Jerry and Jackson came walking around from the back of the building, carrying several rifles and some boxes of ammo.

"They had some nice stuff," Jeb said. "Looks new. We ought to go over to the sporting goods store. I'll bet they just stole them from there."

"You're probably right," Frank said. How far away is it?"

Bug Out! Part 4 – Mortars and Motorhomes

"About four blocks down Main Street. I'll load them in the back of the SUV and take a ride over there, after the Sheriff has been picked up."

"Good," Frank said. Just as he was saying that the ambulance drove past them and pulled back into the park. The paramedics jumped out of the car and pulled the gurney out of the back. They got the Sheriff loaded and into the back in seconds. The ambulance took off, and the Doctor walked across the road to his car, with Earl following him.

"Frank, I'm needed at the hospital, and I'll take Earl so I can make sure his wound is alright. You guys can come pick him up in about an hour....or I can bring him back to the RV Park."

"Alright, Doc, we'll play it by ear. Be careful."

The Doctor nodded, and both men got into his car. They took off.

"Where are the bodies?" asked Jane.

"In the Library, just inside the double doors," Jerry said. "Didn't want any kids to run into them in the street."

"You took the weapons off of them, I trust," Frank said.

"A couple of them had pistols," Jeb said. "And you already know about the hunting rifles."

"Wonder if there is a coroner here that can come get the bodies?"

"Yes, there is," Charlie said. "I've already called them."

"Good," Frank said. "You wanted to go to the gun shop, right? Maybe we should go over there now."

"Frank, I think we should gather up those gun registration records from the Sheriff's station," Jane said. "We don't want those falling into the wrong hands."

"Good idea," Frank said.

"Listen," Jeb said.

The sound of a chopper was approaching quickly.

"Take cover," Charlie said. "We don't know who that is."

Robert Boren

The chopper can into sight. It was the chopper that had taken Officer Simmons away. There was the sound of machine gun fire.

{ 8 }

Let's Hit the Saloon

Machine gun fire filled the air.

"Get into the Sheriff's station," Charlie cried. The all ran for it, and slipped into the door and back away from the windows. Except Jeb.

"Where's Jeb?" asked Jerry?

The machine gun fire was all over the place. It was like somebody was just shooting wild, not trying to hit anything in particular.

"Whoever is manning that chopper has no idea what they are doing," Jackson said. "They should have tagged a couple of us."

Then there was a big bore rifle blast. Then another.

"Jeb," Frank said, rushing off towards the window. He looked out, and saw the chopper starting to reel over to one side, out of control. Jeb rushed in the door.

"Get down, we don't know where that thing is going to crash," he shouted.

"What did you do?"

"I took out the pilot and copilot with this rifle. It's got a nice scope."

They could hear the chopper's blades slowing down, then they could hear the sound of impacts as the rotors hit the street. Then there was a loud crashing sound...breaking fiberglass and metal. The engine stopped. There was silence.

"We'd better get out there," Jeb said. "That didn't land hard enough to kill everybody inside. Somebody was in the back trying to fire that machine gun."

Jeb and Jerry and Jasmine slipped out the door cautiously. Jane was checking her M-16, and Frank his Winchester. They went out, and were followed by Jackson and Charlie. They saw the chopper laying on its side, smoke coming out of the engine compartment. One of the pilots was hanging out of the broken front window. They saw Jerry and Jasmine run out towards the wreckage, trying to avoid any openings in the fuselage. Jeb got behind a car on the street, where he had a good vantage point of the wreckage, including the side window with the broken machine gun barrel sticking out. He brought the rifle up and looked through the scope, ready to fire.

"Let's go over there to the other side," Frank said. "Then we can stop anybody that comes out."

"I'll follow you," Jerry said. "Better let me shoot, though. It would be nice to take somebody alive from this one. That .44 mag will shred them. They might live through it if I shoot them."

"I'm going over next to Jerry," Jackson said.

"Me too," Charlie said. They ran over in a crouch and got next to him.

Frank nodded. They ran down the street, and around the back of the wreckage. They found a cement trash can holder and got behind it, and aimed their rifles at the wreckage.

"Jerry's going in," Frank said.

Jerry got to the opening and looked in. Then he signaled Jackson and Jasmine to come over. The gathered around. Jerry put down his AK-47 and grabbed something. He pulled, and a body came sliding out. Charlie dropped his weapon and leaped over to give him a hand. The person wasn't conscious, but he didn't look dead either. Jasmine held her M-16 on the man while Jerry frisked him. Jackson looked around the wreckage for more people, and then went up front to check out the pilot and copilot. Jerry got finished searching the person, and then turned and gave the thumbs up sign.

"Let's go," Frank said. He and Jane ran over.

"He's still breathing," Jerry said as they all gathered around and looked down at him.

"Geez, he's only a kid," Jane said.

"Pilots?" Frank asked.

"Deader than a doornail," Jackson said. He looked over at Jeb. "How did you manage to tag them both in the forehead while they were in a moving chopper?"

"Damn good scope on this rifle," Jeb said. "And this rifle is smooth as silk. I think I'll try to make a deal with the gun shop when we go over there. I want to keep this sucker. It's better than my rifle. Weatherby....top shelf."

"I have one of those at home," Frank said. "Didn't want to bring it. I was afraid we'd get the guns taken away from us. That's a $2000 dollar rifle, at least."

"Hey, let's focus, folks," Charlie said. "Let's get the Doc over here to look at this kid. I'll call him."

"Yes, you do that," Jane said.

Charlie got on his cellphone and dialed.

"Doc?" he asked.

"Yeah, this Charlie?"

"Yep. Did you hear the chopper?"

"Sure did."

"It was the one that Officer Simmons escaped from. The pilots both bought it, but there was a kid in the back manning the .50 cal. He's still alive. Can you come over?"

"Sure, be there as soon as I can, and I'll send the paramedics now."

"How are the rest of our people?" Charlie asked.

"Earl's fine. He won't be out of action for more than a day or two. The Sheriff is going to make it too. He just needed an IV to get him hydrated again. The Deputy is in bad shape, though."

"Is he going to make it?"

"Probably, but he's going to be in ICU for a few days. I'm sure Simmons thought he was dead."

"Well, get the paramedics out. At least some of us will hang out until you get here."

Will do, Charlie."

Charlie put his phone back in his pocket.

"The doc is going to call the paramedics first," Charlie said. "He'll follow along later."

Everybody looked at him and nodded. The paramedics drove back over in just a couple of minutes. They pulled up next to the wreckage and ran over with their bags.

"Was he thrown out of the chopper?" asked one of the paramedics.

"No, but he probably rattled around inside quite a bit," Jeb said, laughing.

"You think this is funny?" the paramedic asked.

"He's the enemy," Jeb said. "I shot the pilot and co-pilot, and that's what brought down the chopper. This kid was firing that .50 cal at us before I made it crash."

"Oh," the paramedic said sheepishly. "So why didn't you just shoot him?"

"We need information," Charlie said.

The paramedic nodded, and got to work.

The Doctor got there in a couple of minutes, and trotted over to the wreckage. He looked at the boy, who was now on the gurney, ready to load in the ambulance.

"Concussion," the Doctor said. "He'll probably be alright, but he needs to go to the hospital."

"Is there a jail ward there?" asked Charlie. "We don't want this kid getting up and walking away. He's an enemy combatant."

"Well, kind of. We have a room that locks from the outside. We could put him in there."

"He might be dangerous," Jerry said. "We should cuff him to the bed. I saw a pair of cuffs in the Sheriff's station. I'll go get them."

The Doctor nodded. Jerry took off running, and was back in a minute. He cuffed the kid to the gurney, and handed the keys to the paramedic.

"Alright, we're off," the Doctor said. The ambulance took off down the road, with the doctor behind it.

"Now what?" asked Frank.

"Let's go gather up those gun registration forms," Jane said.

Frank nodded, and they went back into the Sheriff's station.

"I'll call the coroner about those two deputies in the jail," Charlie said. He fished his cellphone out of his pocket and walked away as he dialed.

Jeb looked at Jackson. "Let's take these rifles back to the Sporting Goods store," he said. "I put the guns in the back."

Jackson nodded, and the two of them got into the SUV and drove off. Charlie and Jasmine and Jerry walked into the Sheriff's station.

"Coroner's on the way," Charlie said. "Wonder if these guys have family in town?"

"Probably," Jasmine said. "So sad."

"I'm going to mop up this blood," Jerry said. "I saw a mop and bucket in the back."

Jane and Frank walked out of the back with a file storage box.

"This is all of the gun registration files," Jane said. "What should we do with them?"

"Burn them," Jerry said.

"You know, that's not a bad idea," Frank said. "Let's do it."

"Isn't that illegal?" Jane asked.

"Who cares?" Jerry asked.

"We could take them down to the Sporting Goods store," Jane said.

"That's probably the first place that the enemy looked for them," Jerry said. "And I'll bet the folks who run that store are all dead."

"I'm afraid of that too," Charlie said. "Burn em."

"Alright," Jane said.

"There's a 55 gallon drum behind this building," Frank said. "Let's use that."

Frank carried the box around and dumped it into the drum. Charlie pulled out a book of matches and started one of the papers, and then dropped it in. The paper caught, and soon there was a big flame extending a foot out of the drum. Jane stood by and watched, and then walked next to Frank and put her arm around his waist.

"I guess it's for the best," she said. "Look, here comes Jeb and Jackson." She pointed to the SUV slowly driving up to them. They pulled over to the side of the road and got out of the SUV.

"What's that?" asked Jeb.

"Gun registration records," Charlie said.

"Good thinking. Somebody went through all of the paperwork in the Sporting Goods store too. There's bodies in the store. Looks like the owner, a young kid who was probably clerk, and somebody who looks like a customer. I just kept the rifles, and grabbed a bunch of ammo."

"I was afraid of that," Charlie said.

An older woman walked up cautiously. She had on a long dress, and her gray hair was tied up behind her head. She was a handsome woman with a pretty smile.

"Jeb?" she asked.

"Stella, is that you?" Jeb asked. "I ain't seen you in a coon's age. Was that you behind that window over there?"

"I didn't think you recognized me," she said, with a calm smile. "I'm old now."

"You're still beautiful, Stella," Jeb said. He walked over and gave her a hug.

"You live in town?" Jane asked. "I'm Jane, by the way."

"Yes, Jane, I still live here," she said. "Most of the people who live around the center of town are about my age. Some of them are in worse shape. Luckily the Doctor is still around to look in. The younger people who lived around here are mostly gone, except the ones that work in the hospital and the little hotel and saloon."

"Saloon?" Jackson said. "It still open?"

"Yes, Clarence is still running the place."

"Clarence?" Jeb asked. "That old SOB is still alive?"

"Yes, Jeb, he's in good shape for an old guy, too."

"Did you know the Deputies?" asked Jane.

"I knew the Sheriff's nephew. Great kid but way too gentle for the job. The other two got hired from outside of town."

"Well, I guess that's good. They are both dead in the jail."

"Oh, no. Those poor boys," Stella said.

"Are there a lot of people who live outside of town?" asked Frank.

"Yes, there are homes all over the place. Lots of rednecks. I'm surprised they didn't attack these folks."

"Any of them in the militia?" asked Charlie.

"A few were, but they all left, from what I heard," she said. "Nutcases."

Charlie's phone rang. He pulled it out of his pocket.

"Hi, Doc. Earl ready to pick up yet?"

"Yes, you can come get him any time. The prisoner woke up, too. He's a handful. You call the coroner about those two bodies in the jail?"

"Yes, I called them. They ought to be here any minute. There's several dead people in the sporting goods store also. I'll let them know."

"Alright. You guys want to come down here?"

"Sure, after the coroner gets here," Charlie said. "How's the Sheriff?"

"He's good. He's already flirting with the nurses. He perked up considerably when he found out that his nephew is going to be alright."

"Yeah, I got the impression that the Sheriff thought he was dead."

"He did," the Doctor said. "I'd better get going. See you in a while."

"Thanks, Doc. You've been such a big help."

"Don't mention it," he said.

Charlie put the phone back in his pocket.

"Earl?" Jackson said.

"He's in good shape, and we can pick him up any time. Sheriff's recovering quickly as well, and our prisoner is awake."

"So we are going over there after the coroner gets here?" Frank asked.

"Yep, but not all of us have to go over."

"I should call the Major and ask him what we should do with the prisoner," Frank said.

"Good idea," Jeb said. "I think I'd like to take a quick walk over to the Saloon. Could use a beer."

"I heard that," Jackson said.

"I'll go with you," Stella said. "So old Clarence doesn't shoot you when you walk in the door."

"Don't drink too much," Charlie said. "We don't know what's going to happen around here. We might not be finished yet."

Jeb nodded, and walked off with Stella and Jackson.

Frank went over to the squad car and picked up the radio microphone.

"Major Hobbs, you there?"

"I was getting worried about you guys. What's happening?"

"Mop up. We just talked to the Doctor over at the hospital. Earl's good enough to come back with us. The Sheriff's recovering, and the Deputy as well, but they'll be in the hospital for a little longer…especially the Deputy. Oh, and we know where that chopper is."

"Where?"

"I'm looking at its smoking wreckage right now," Frank said.

"Really?"

"Really. It arrived about fifteen minutes after the battle was over, and opened up on us with the .50 cal. We took cover in the Sheriff's station, except for Jeb. He took the pilot and co-pilot out with a hunting rifle. Head shots. Amazing."

"Anybody survive?"

"Yes, the kid who was manning the .50 cal is alive. He has a concussion, but otherwise seems to be fine. We have him restrained in the hospital, but it's not very secure. What should we do with him?"

"How about the jail?"

"That's what we were thinking, but I don't think we want to be responsible for him very long."

"Gotcha," the Major said. "I'll call the CO."

"Alright. We're going over to the hospital as soon as the coroner gets here."

"Coroner?"

"Yes, the other two deputies were hung by the enemy. They're inside the jail cell."

"Dammit."

"That's not all. They also hit the sporting goods store. There's three bodies in there."

"Did they take a lot of weapons?"

"I don't know," Frank said. "The snipers on the roof had some nice Weatherby hunting rifles with scopes. Jeb used one of them to take out the chopper. He kept them after he saw that the folks in the store were all dead, and he grabbed a bunch of ammo too."

"Good. Anything else?"

"Yeah, the enemy ransacked the store and the Sheriff's station. They found gun registration forms in the Sheriff's station, and were getting ready to take them away."

"Interesting," the Major said. "What did you do with them?"

"We burned them," Frank said.

"Good. I'll get back to you after I've talked to the CO."

"Alright. If you can't get to me on the radio, try my cellphone."

"That reminds me, you might want to take a look at the cell tower. Maybe there's a way to make it more secure."

"Excellent idea, Major. Forgot all about that. Talk to you soon."

Frank hooked the radio microphone back onto its holder and shut the door to the squad car. He walked back over to the group, just as the coroner's wagon rolled down the street and parked.

"It's the meat wagon," Jerry said. Jasmine rolled her eyes.

"Sick, man," Frank said, chuckling as he walked up. "The major just reminded me of something. We should go check out that cell tower, and see if there's anything we can do to make it more secure."

"I'm with you on that," Jerry said. "Oh, and I mopped up all that blood, so the coroner can get in and out easier."

"Good," Charlie said. "I'll get the coroner going, and meet you guys down at the saloon. Then we can go over to the hospital."

"Where is the saloon, again?" Jerry asked.

"It's on the street that runs behind these buildings…..to the north. The cell tower is on the way…about a block this side of where the saloon and hotel are."

"Alright," Frank said. "Charlie, will you drive the squad car over after you're done here? We'll take the SUV over to the cell tower."

"Sure," Charlie said. "I'll lock up the Sheriff's station after we're done, and take the keys over to the Sheriff when we hit the hospital."

Bug Out! Part 4 – Mortars and Motorhomes

"C'mon, girls, lets go," Frank said. Jane and Jasmine nodded, and they all climbed into the SUV.

"Hey Frank, Jasmine is an expert on cellular technology," Jerry said. "Good thing we have her here."

"Excellent," Frank said. Jane looked up at him.

"I hope we are almost done. I'm tired, and I'll bet Lucy is going crazy sitting in that motor home all by herself"

"She has Mr. Wonderful to keep her company," Frank said. "You and Jasmine saved our butts big time."

Jane smiled and put her hand on his thigh as he drove.

"I'll say," Jerry said.

"Good, then you won't be making us wait while you guys go fight anymore, right?" Jasmine asked.

"Nope," Jerry said. "At least until I have you knocked up."

"Jerry! You're as bad as mom," Jasmine said.

"There's the cell tower," Frank said, pointing. He pulled the SUV over to the side of the road, and they all got out and walked over to it.

"Crap, look at this," Jasmine said. "They just barely re-connected it. That isn't going to last. If somebody steps on it here, it will come apart."

"What do we need to fix it?" asked Jane.

"Some new connectors," Jasmine said. "And I'd like to have some kind of conduit over it, like that." She pointed at the original conduit that was ripped open and tossed to the side.

"Wonder if there is a good hardware store in town that is still open?" Frank asked.

"I'll tell you what," Jasmine said. "I can jury rig this thing so it will hold for a while. Then we can ask the folks in the saloon if there is a place we can get what we need."

"Okay," Jerry said. "Tell me how I can help."

The couple got to work. Frank looked around. He could see the Saloon. It was only a block away.

"Jane, let's walk over to the saloon," he said. Jane nodded.

"We'll see you over there in a few minutes," Jerry said.

Frank's phone rang. He pulled it out of his pocket.

"Frank here," he said.

"Frank, it's Hobbs. The CO is coming over there. He'll be in a larger helicopter, with a detachment of men. It will be a dual rotor job. Chinook. Ought to be arriving in about twenty minutes."

"Excellent," Frank said. "Jerry and Jasmine are working on the cell tower now. It's in bad shape. We need some parts, but she can jury rig it for the short term. We're going over to the Hotel and Saloon. Hopefully we can find out if there's a store around that carries what we need."

"Alright, Frank, talk to you soon." Frank put the phone back in his pocket.

They were almost up to the Saloon. It was an old west looking building with a wood sidewalk in front of it, and swinging saloon doors. The main doors were closed behind it.

"Something's not right," Frank whispered. "Why would those inner doors be closed?"

"Uh oh," Jane said. "Look at the Class C over there." She pointed, and took off the safety on her M-16. Frank did the same on his Winchester.

"Let's sneak up and look in a window," Frank whispered. The crept forward, and crawled up onto the wooden sidewalk. Frank stuck his head up for a split second, then brought it back down, a worried look on his face."

"What?" Jane whispered.

"Lewis is in there, holding a gun on Jeb, Jackson and Stella."

{ 9 }

Chester Saves the Day

Jane and Frank crouched, watching the front of the saloon.

"What do we do now?" asked Jane, looking frightened.

"If I know Jeb, he's about three steps ahead of this creep," Frank said.

"Jerry and Jasmine are going to show up any second," Jane said.

"I'll text Jerry now." Frank pulled out his phone and sent the text.

"Jeb and others held in Saloon by Lewis. Can see them through the window. Be carefu.l"

"Got it. Jeb always has other weapons on him. A diversion would help."

"I've got an idea."

"Shoot."

"Sneak up and shoot tires on the Class C."

"Then what?"

"Jane and I will tag anybody who comes out, and then go in."

"Good, be there in a minute. I'll call Charlie."

"Good, thanks."

Frank snuck back over to Jane.

"Jerry and Jasmine are going to sneak over here and shoot out the tires on that class C. You and I are going to be ready to shoot Lewis if he comes out. Hopefully the diversion will give Jeb or Jackson an opening to do something in there."

"Risky plan. What if there are other people here with Lewis?"

"If they aren't ours, blast em," Frank said.

"Wish we knew what the Saloon keeper looked like."

"Shit, forgot about him. He's really old. I think it's unlikely that an elderly man is with Lewis's folks, so don't shoot any really old folks unless they are shooting at you."

"Great advice…..don't shoot old people," Jane said, smirking. "Look, here they come,"

"Good. Why don't you sneak over behind that tree….you can see the front doors and windows."

"Where are you going?"

"Back up on the porch, so I can see in the window when things start up," Frank said.

"That's pretty exposed."

"I can roll off of this sidewalk quickly if I have to. And I have you to cover me, and Jerry and Jasmine."

"Alright," she said, and she ran in a crouched position over to the big oak tree off to the right side in front of the building. When she was in place, Frank gave a thumbs up sign to Jerry. He got on one knee and aimed at the Class C rig. Jasmine did the same, about four feet away from him. Then they both fired, and hitting the two front tires of the rig. It slumped down in front. Two men came flying out of the door of the coach, and were hit immediately by Jasmine's M-16.

Frank looked into the Saloon. Lewis turned around, and Jeb leaped at him with a bowie knife in his hand. He stabbed Lewis before he could react. The gun fell out of his hand. Jackson grabbed his gun off of the bar, and tossed Jeb's gun to him as well. Frank started to get up, when a shot came from inside the Class C. Then another. He dived off the wooden sidewalk, into the planter below.

Jerry and Jasmine ran for cover behind a tree on the other side of the building, and both of them shot back at the Class C rig.

"Stay down Jane!" Frank yelled. Then he saw movement behind the Class C. It was Chester, sneaking towards the door with his usual limp. He made eye contact with Frank and held up his hand. There was a grenade in it. Frank nodded. Chester pulled the pin, then yanked open the screen door on the rig and tossed it in. Then he jumped to the ground and tried to crawl away. The Class C exploded. Chester was way too close.

"Shit, Chester," Frank yelled. He ran over and grabbed his shoulders, and pulled him away from the burning hulk. He had glass and metal and wood stuck in his back, and a bloody gash on the back of his head. Jane ran over.

"Oh, no, is he dead?" she asked.

"He doesn't look good. Let's drag him further away. The propane tank is going to blow,"

They each grabbed one of his arms and dragged him away from the Class C. Then there was another explosion, and the Class C lifted off of the ground and settled back down. The heat was intense.

Jeb and Jackson ran out of the saloon.

"Oh, no, is that Chester?" cried Jeb. He ran down to help Frank and Jane. They brought him up the porch steps and into the saloon just as Charlie rolled up in the Squad car. They laid him on a bench just inside the door. Jerry and Jasmine got up onto the wooden sidewalk, and nodded to each other. They turned facing outward and stood watch, just in case there were more militia folks around.

"Oh, no, what did Chester do?" cried Charlie as he ran up. He was openly weeping, looking at Chester's lifeless body.

"He saved us," Frank said. "He tossed a grenade into that Class C rig. We were taking fire. Sounded like there was three people in there shooting at us."

"I'm calling the Doc," Charlie said, wiping the tears out of his eyes.

"Dammit, Chester," Jeb cried, tears streaming out of his eyes. Jane went over next to Frank and hugged him, sobbing.

"The Doc is on his way," Charlie said.

Stella walked over. She was shaking and crying.

"I was looking forward to catching up with you, you old fool," she said to Chester, tears in her eyes.

"What happened in here?" Frank asked.

"Well, we got here and the place was deserted, but wide open," Jeb said. "We started looking around, and found old Clarence lying behind the bar. His throat was cut ear to ear with his own knife. That one." He pointed to the bowie knife sticking in Lewis's back. "Lewis got the drop on us."

"Bastards," Charlie said. He was still crying.

"You guys went back a long way, didn't you?" Jane asked.

"Yeah," Jeb said. "Chester was the oldest of us. My folks thought he was a bad influence. He was always coming up with some stupid plan or other. He was a dashing guy in his youth, that's for sure. He took Charlie and me under his wing, and we had a lot of good times with him."

The Doctor came in, and looked at everybody. Then he looked closely at Chester.

"There isn't anything I can do for him," he said. "That head wound. Nobody could survive that. How did this happen?"

"Chester tossed a grenade into that burning motor home out there," Frank said. "He couldn't get far enough away before it blew."

"Geez," the Doctor said. "I take it he saved you folks."

"Yep," Charlie said.

"Listen," Jeb said. Everybody hushed up. There was the sound of a helicopter approaching.

"That's probably the CO," Frank said. "Right on time, too."

Bug Out! Part 4 – Mortars and Motorhomes

"Major Hobbs told you he was coming?" asked the Doctor.

"Yes," Frank said. "Should be a large double rotor chopper."

"Probably a Chinook," Jerry said.

"I hear more than one," Jeb said. "We'd better go take a look."

Frank, Jeb, and Jackson stepped out and looked up. They could see the choppers heading for the park in front of the Sheriff's station. It was a Chinook, and two Apache attack helicopters were flying close by.

"Let's get back over to the Sheriff's station," Frank said. Everybody except for the Doctor and Stella piled into the squad car and SUV. They got to the Sheriff's station just as the Chinook set down.

"Wow, look at the size of that thing," Jasmine said as Frank parked the SUV. Jerry nodded. Charlie pulled the squad car up next to the SUV

The back door on the Chinook opened up like a ramp, and about ten men ran out, M-16s in hand, looking in every direction. One of them saw the SUV and the Squad car pull up, and pointed. Soon the two vehicles were surrounded by troops, all pointing guns at them. A General walked over to the vehicles.

"Which one of you is Frank Johnson?" he asked.

"I am, sir," Frank said from the driver's seat of the SUV.

"Stand down, gentlemen," the General said. The troops lowered their weapons, and Frank slowly got out. The General walked up and shook his hand.

"I'm General Walker," he said. "I've heard good things about you and your friends."

"Thank you sir," Frank said. The rest of the group got out of the SUV and squad car.

"I'm General Walker. What's your names?"

"I'm Jane," she said as she got next to Frank.

"Jackson."

"Charlie."

"Jeb."

"Ah," the General said. "So you're the famous Jeb. Major Dobbs is very impressed." Jeb nodded, looking a little embarrassed.

"Jerry," said Jerry.

"And Jerry, heard good things about you too. Former military, right?"

"Yes sir. This is my wife."

"Jasmine," she said.

"Well, it's really nice to meet you. Is that all of you?"

"Earl is in the hospital, along with the Sheriff and his Deputy," Frank said. "We just lost a person. His name was Chester. He's responsible for that smoke over there."

"The major said you guys were here to rescue the Sheriff from this 'Officer Simmons' character. I take it you were successful?"

"Yes, except for losing Chester," Jeb said.

"What happened to him?"

"We were taking fire from that Class C motorhome that Lewis was driving," Frank said. "Chester snuck over to it and tossed in a grenade. He moves pretty slow, and couldn't get far enough away from the blast."

"Sorry to hear that," General Walker said. "So Lewis showed up back here, huh? We've been trying to find him, but there are a lot of places to hide around here. Is he alive?"

"Nope, I stabbed him with a bowie knife," Jeb said.

"Damn," the General said. "Bow and Arrows and Bowie Knifes too? Were you born in the right century?" He chuckled.

"Probably not, I reckon," Jeb said. "I do like this Weatherby, though. Nothing like this back in the old days." He held it out, and the General took a closer look.

"Yes, that is one beautiful weapon," he said. "I hear you have a prisoner for me."

Bug Out! Part 4 – Mortars and Motorhomes

"Yes, sir," Frank said. "The kid who was manning the .50 cal on that chopper over there."

"Good. Where is he?"

"Over at the hospital," Frank said. "We were about ready to go over there. Want to join us?"

"Yes, but give me a minute," he said. He looked over at his Corporal. "Back my Humvee out of there, Corporal Barnes."

"Yes sir," he said, and he trotted back to the Chinook. Soon the Humvee was backing down the ramp. It was a battle version, with a .50 cal mounted in the back. He drove it up next to the SUV and Squad car.

"Alright, folks, lead the way," General Walker said.

"Will do, but we should go by way of the Saloon and get the Doctor."

"I'll just call him, Frank," Charlie said. "He's on speed dial, I'm afraid."

"Alright, you do that, and then lead the way," Frank said. "I don't even know where the hospital is."

"Will do," Charlie said. He pulled out his cell phone and dialed.

"Doc?"

"Yes, Charlie."

"Can you meet us at the Hospital? The General wants to talk to the prisoner."

"Of course, be there in a minute."

"Thanks, Doc," Charlie said. He shoved his phone back into his pocket.

"Alright, let's go," he said. He jumped into the squad car and drove slowly down the street. The SUV and Humvee followed.

The Hospital was on the outskirts of town. It was a two story building that was surprisingly large for the size of the town. Charlie pulled into one of the parking stalls up front, and the Humvee pulled in next to it. Frank parked the SUV in an open spot opposite of the front row. Everybody got out of their vehicles, and were collecting up in front of the wide double doors when the Doctor drove in. He parked, and then walked up to the group.

"Hi, all," he said. The General walked up to him and extended his hand.

"General Walker, Doc. Good to meet you. Thanks for doing such a good job patching up Lieutenant James."

"You are quite welcome, Sir," he said. "Follow me."

He walked towards the door, and both sides slid open. Everybody went through to the lobby.

"There's a conference room over to the left there," the Doctor said. "Why don't you all take a seat in there, and I'll get some coffee brought in. Then I'll take the General back to see the prisoner."

"Coffee sounds great," Jeb said.

They all went into the conference room. It had a long table, with twelve chairs on each side and one chair on each end. There was also a row of chairs along the back wall, and a large credenza on the opposite wall. After a few minutes, an orderly came in with a cart. As the group all sat down, the coffee maker and cups and condiments were set up.

"Ready to go, General?" asked the Doc.

"Sure," he said. "Maybe we should take a representative of the group back there with us. Who would you guys like?"

"Frank," Jeb said. Charlie and Jerry nodded in approval, and then the rest did.

"Ok, Frank, guess you're it," General Walker said. Frank kissed Jane on the forehead, and joined the Doc and the General as they left the room.

"Is the prisoner badly wounded?" asked General Walker as they went down the long hallway.

"No, not really," the Doctor said. "He had a concussion, but I don't think it's serious."

Bug Out! Part 4 – Mortars and Motorhomes

"Good, so I could take him with us without causing a problem?"

"I don't see why not," the Doctor said. "We don't want to keep him longer than needed. I don't want any of his friends shooting their way in here to rescue him."

"You have any armed security here?" Frank asked.

"No, not really, and that's a bigger problem now since the Sheriff and his surviving Deputy are both out of action."

"I'd like to chat with the Sheriff before we leave, if he's up to it," the General said.

"No problem," the Doc said, with a smirk. "It will take the pressure off of the nurses for a few minutes. He's a terrible flirt, that Sheriff."

"Good sign that he's going to be okay," Frank said. "We need him back in fighting trim. Jeb is getting all the attention for his prowess, but I'll never forget the Sheriff picking off Islamic fighters running at him 200 yards out with his bolt action hunting rifle. That was something to see."

"Heard about that from Major Hobbs. You guys have an impressive team," the General said.

"We've been lucky too, though, and your Major has saved us more than once," Frank said. "Hobbs walks on water in my book."

"Yes, Major Hobbs is one of our best," the General said.

"Here's our 'prison ward', such as it is," the Doc said, laughing. He unlocked the door and they all went in. The prisoner looked over at them, and then spit on the floor.

"Hi, Son," the General said.

"I'm not your son," he said sarcastically.

"What militia group were you in?" General Walker asked.

"You can take a guess. I'm not telling you shit, asshole."

"Well, he seems to be in decent health," the General said. "Full of piss and vinegar, isn't he?"

"Jeb wanted to blow him away," Frank said. "Maybe that would have been the best idea."

{ 109 }

"You stupid sheep," the prisoner said. "Your days are numbered."

"What, you mean you still have a few people left?" Frank said. He laughed.

The General looked over at Frank…..his look told him to shut up.

"That's right, bow to the 'General', Frank," the prisoner said mockingly.

"How do you know his name?" asked the Doc.

"Everybody in the movement knows who Frank is. He murdered two of our best. They were only trying to help him out."

"Make that four as of this morning," Frank said.

The General gave him the look again.

"Sorry, General Walker. Maybe I shouldn't be in here."

"No worries," the General said. He turned to the Doc. "I'll send a detachment of men over here to pick up the prisoner. We'll take him back to base with us."

"Fine with me," the Doc said. "We'll be glad to be rid of him."

"Good, then I think we are done here for now," he said. "See you soon."

"I'll see you hanged," the prisoner said.

"Take your best shot," the General said as they left the room. The Doc locked the door back up.

"Belligerent little son of a bitch, isn't he," the General said. "I doubt we'll get much out of him, but we'll make a big deal about having him at the base so word spreads far and wide. That should keep his inbred friends from trying to hit the town looking for him."

"I'd appreciate that, General," the Doc said. "We're the only hospital still operating in this area. It would be a big problem to lose it."

They continued down the hallway towards the conference room.

"This was the first major action the town has seen, wasn't it?" the General asked.

"Yes, that's correct," the Doc said. "They've been messing with the RV Park a lot, though."

"We think that's because we have a growing assortment of their weapons and supplies," Frank said.

"Well, there's another reason, and you just heard it in there," General Walker said. "They are using you folks as a rallying cry. You are the people who murdered their precious leaders. You have become their own sort of Nazi Blood Flag."

"Nazi Blood Flag?" Frank asked.

"Yeah, it was a flag that was at the failed 1923 coup attempt. It was used to soak up the blood of dead Nazis at that event. The Nazis used it in ceremonies for years, to rally the faithful."

"Great," Frank said, shaking his head.

"We need to talk about that and some other things," the General said. "I was going to suggest going back to the RV Park for that, but perhaps we could use this nice conference room instead. I can smell the coffee from here."

They walked through the door of the conference room. Everybody hushed as they came in. Earl was with them. Frank nodded to him as he walked through the door, with a big smile on his face. Earl smiled back at him warmly.

"Sit down everybody, and we'll talk," the General said. He went over to the credenza and got himself a cup of coffee. Frank and the Doc did as well, and they all sat down.

"First of all, I'd like to say how impressed I am with your group," the General said. "I've been getting reports on your situation and your actions ever since Major Hobbs and Lieutenant James first arrived. You are the best of American society, and it gives me great hope when I see you rally to the fight."

"We've been very impressed with your team as well," Jerry said. "Major Hobbs, Lieutenant James, and your new Sergeant, and the privates too. Top notch."

"Thanks, Jerry, I'm proud of them too," he said. "I've got two things to discuss with you."

He walked back over to the coffee area and added a little more cream to his coffee.

"Strong stuff," he said, laughing. "First of all, I'd like to have permission to keep Major Hobbs and his detachment at the RV Park for the time being. I'd also like to augment his force to replace the people we lost there."

"I think all of us in this room are for that," Charlie said, "but the park belongs to Hilda. We'd have to get her okay. I'd be shocked if she would have a problem, though."

"Can you be sure that the replacement troops aren't going to turn?" asked Jerry.

"We think so," the General said. "There was an intelligence breakthrough on that a couple of days ago, and we were able to pinpoint who the remaining plants were. They're all in the brig now. I'm not going to lie to you and tell you we are 100% sure we got them all, though. We still need to be careful. We'll only bring longer-service assets into the RV Park this time. We think that will protect against any residual issues."

"Well, that's good news," Jeb said.

"What else?" asked Jerry.

"Here is the difficult part of the conversation," the General said.

Jerry shot a glance over to Frank and Jeb.

"Go on," Frank said.

"This area has become very dangerous, because it is where the Northern and Southern branches of the enemy forces are attempting to link up. They can't go east, because of the Rocky mountains on the north end of that corridor, and New Mexico on the south. Texas is helping New Mexico to mop things up now that they've stopped the enemy in the south."

"Does that mean we can move east to get out of here?" asked Jane.

Bug Out! Part 4 – Mortars and Motorhomes

"Maybe, but let me finish," the General said. "The enemy would like come down through Idaho into Nevada and use that as a staging point to attack California, but the terrain there is just too difficult, and forces in California are now starting to focus on the eastern border of that state and on into Nevada."

"What happened up in Washington State?" asked Jerry.

"That was a real blood bath, but the local forces and the citizenry won. The enemy won't be trying to come through there again. They are coming down through Montana and Wyoming and into Utah….and right down our throats."

"Don't we have Arizona locked up now?" asked Jackson.

"Yes and no," the General said. "We control all of the cities, but there are a lot of forces hiding around the Grand Canyon area. We aren't going to bomb around there, so we are having to root them out with ground forces."

"Where do these guys think they are going to go?" asked Earl.

"Well, that's the real question," the General said. "They can't go east in large numbers. They can't go west in large numbers. We are now starting to pull assets from Northern California into Idaho and Montana, so pretty soon they will be cut off from coming down through there or even escaping back to Canada. The Canadians are making real headway against these folks too. We think that they are going to rally in Utah and then try to break into much smaller forces and cause as much damage as they can. They know they're essentially on a suicide mission now. They can't even go back to Mexico at this point."

"So you are telling me that this war is close to over," Jane said.

"Yes, we are getting there, but it's going to be a long bloody process to get everything cleaned up in this corridor, and there's very intense fighting still going on down in Mexico. I need to focus on this area and make sure that enemy strength doesn't grow, and that the enemy can't freely escape into the rest of the country, even in small groups."

"There's something hanging out there that you really don't want to bring up," Jerry said.

"Yes. There is a rallying cry that the southern forces are using to help hold themselves together, and it's the reason this particular area continues to get hit. I need to remove that rallying cry."

"What is it?" asked Jeb.

"You, Frank and Jane, Jerry and Jasmine, Charley, Earl, and Jackson. They have made you all out to be the devil incarnate, and as long as you are around here, there will be problems around the RV Park and the town too."

"So what are you proposing?" asked Frank

{ 10 }

A Wedding and a Funeral

Frank looked the General in the eye, waiting for a response. Jane put her hand over his on the conference room table. The others were all sitting around the conference table, looking at General Walker. You could hear a pin drop.

"Do you want to relocate us or protect us?" Jane asked.

"I want to relocate you guys, and then spread the news around," the General said. "It won't get rid of the enemy here, but it will move the focus away from the town and surrounding area. Without you guys as the big villains, there are some people in the local militia that will probably just sink back into the woodwork and give up. It may break the alliance between the southern militia and the Islamists."

"You're thinking that a lot of these militia kooks are only staying in the fight to get revenge on us?" Jeb asked. "Sounds a little thin to me."

"Believe it or not, that's what our sources are telling us," the General said. "The good news, though, is that the southern militia is holding on by a thread, and you guys have just taken out their two strongest leaders."

"Lewis and Officer Simmons?" Jackson asked.

"Yes," General Walker said. "If we can get you out of the picture, they lose the most important propaganda tool they have left. They are teetering over the edge now, and that might just push them over."

"Who's running that group now?" Jerry asked

"We aren't sure. It's either somebody from the Yuma core, or somebody from the Williams core. We do know one thing, though."

"What's that?" Earl asked.

"The militia members are a big help to the Islamists, because they know the territory and the people. If we can break that alliance, it's going to leave the Islamists adrift, and we will be able to mop them up much easier."

"Why the heck are the militia folks helping these guys, anyway?" Jackson asked. "I knew some of these folks. They hate people from the Middle East. Frankly, they hate anybody that isn't like them."

"The militia leaders have been successful at duping their membership into thinking that the U.S. government is the biggest danger. They thought that the Islamists would help them overthrow the government, and then they would simply take control and squash them."

"That sounds pretty stupid to me," Jasmine said.

"Well, yes and no," Jerry said. "These Islamists are true believers, and that keeps them from being rational. The militia probably thinks they will start pissing off the citizens after the U.S. government is gone. You know, the old 'convert or die' routine that backfired on them in California. The militia probably thinks that they can turn the people against them at that point, lead the fight to take them out, and look like heroes."

"That's as stupid as the BS that Manson was trying to sell to the hippies," Jeb said.

Jerry looked at Jeb and grinned.

"You know it and I know it, Jeb. But these folks aren't exactly mental giants."

"Probably why our little rag-tag outfit has been able to beat them back every time they've come against us," Frank said. "Alright, General, we know what you would like. What are the details?"

"I can't force you folks to go along with this, so let's start with that," he said.

"Sure about that?" asked Jerry.

"Yes, we are not under martial law in this territory."

"So are you thinking you could caravan with us to someplace else?" asked Charlie. "A long line of slow-moving motor homes is going to be an easy target."

"I wouldn't advise that," General Walker said.

"What would you advise, General?" asked Jeb.

"I want to airlift all of you out. I'd suggest someplace to the east....perhaps Texas, but any of the lower Midwest states or the southern states would do, as long as they aren't right on the coast."

"What about our rigs?" asked Charlie. "And the RV Park?"

"I suggest you leave your rigs sitting where they are."

"But those are our homes," Jerry said. "A lot of us are full timers. Everything we own is in these rigs."

"We can't do a lot about the contents in your rigs. You can take what you can carry in a few boxes. As for the rigs themselves, Uncle Sam will take care of that. If you help the government out with this, you will be provided with brand new rigs when you get to your destination. And you can pick up your old rigs here after the war is over, assuming they are still intact."

"Crap," Jeb said. "I was just about through the shakedown on my rig. Not sure I want to go through that again." Earl and Jerry shook their heads in agreement.

"I know it's an inconvenience for some of you," General Walker said. "Staying at the RV Park might result in you not living through this war, though. You might want to consider that in your thinking.

Not all of you have new rigs, either, from what I've heard. Some of you could use an upgrade."

"That's true, but not all rigs are created equal," Jeb said. "Are you going to stick somebody who has invested in a DP with some el cheapo entry level gasser?"

"What's a DP?" asked the General.

"Diesel Pusher," Frank said. "Big bucks. Some of them cost several hundred grand. Entry level gassers start at about 70 grand."

"Oh," the General said. "I can't guarantee exactly what you'll get, folks. Sorry. I doubt that we'll be giving you pieces of crap, though. They will be new serviceable units, good enough to live in. And don't forget, you will still own your original rigs. They have as much of a chance of surviving with you gone as they would if you stayed around here. Probably more, since you won't be drawing the bad guys over anymore. Most of you have insurance too, right?"

"Well, maybe so, maybe not," Jeb said. "But I ain't stupid. This is probably going to be our best choice. Every time we kill off a bunch of these cretins, they just send more. We won't keep winning forever. We've been lucky so far."

"What's the strength of the enemy in this corridor, General?" asked Jerry.

"That's classified," the General said.

"Bullshit," Jerry said. "We are leveling with you. Now you level with us. We're on the same side. We need the info to make our decision."

General Walker looked down, thinking. Then he looked out at the group.

"OK, I'll tell you what I know, but if this gets out of the room, I'll be coming after all of you folks, and you'll land in the brig." He had a stern look on his face. Everybody in the room nodded yes, looking at each other. There was a hush in the room.

"We agree," Charlie said.

"Alright. There are over two hundred thousand Islamist fighters between the Canadian and Mexican borders in this corridor. There are also about three thousand in the militia."

"Holy shit," Frank said. "How did so many get here?"

"A lot snuck over the northern and southern borders before we locked it down.....before the war started, even," the General said. "There are also a huge number that fled from the west and the east, after they were defeated in California and Texas."

"I hope the jerks in Washington are proud of themselves," Jerry said.

"Let's just say that this debacle has ended a few careers," the General said.

Jane looked up at Frank, and then over at the General.

"Would it be possible for us to go home to California?" she asked.

"I'm sorry, but we aren't letting anybody back into California at this time," the General said.

"Why not?" Jane asked.

"It's stable, and a base of operation for this half of the country. Since there's not a good enough way to tell the good guys from the bad guys right now, the folks in DC have just sealed it up for everybody. Nobody gets in."

"Our son is in there," Jane said. There were tears in her eyes.

"Remember, he enlisted," Frank said softly. "He isn't just hanging around there. I'm more worried about our daughter."

"Sarah," Jane said. "General, our daughter is in Boise, we think. What is going on there now? Is it safe?"

"Yes, we stopped the flow into that area," the General said. "Nowhere is completely safe, but Boise is a whole lot safer than here."

"We need to get her on the phone," Frank said. "She might have gone back to Portland by now."

"Portland is pretty safe, too," the General said. "I'd rather be in Boise, though. There's no harbor nearby. If you can get ahold of your daughter and she's still in Boise, tell her to stay there."

"Well, folks, we've got some thinking to do," Charlie said. "Why don't we all go back to the park and discuss it?"

"Yes, do that, folks. I'll give you a couple of days to think about it," the General said. "And remember that the info I gave you guys about the strength of the enemy is classified."

"We can say that the strength is such that it makes it unsafe to stay, correct?" asked Jasmine.

"Yes, just don't say the actual numbers," the General said. He rose to leave. "Thanks for your time, folks. I'm going to go get the detachment over here to pick up our prisoner. I'll be at the RV Park this evening." He put down his empty coffee cup and left the conference room.

There was silence for a few moments. Everybody just looked at each other.

"What are we going to do about Chester?" asked Jane.

"The coroner should have picked up his body by now," Charlie said. "I called him on the way over here."

"Are we going to have a memorial?" asked Jasmine.

"I think we should," Jeb said.

"I agree," Charlie said. "Let's talk about it when we get back. I'm not looking forward to telling Hilda."

"Yeah, I could imagine," Jeb said. "You aren't going to leave without her, are you?"

"No," Charlie said. "I'll have to convince her to go too. I can't leave her behind. I'd stay rather than do that."

Jeb walked over and patted him on the back.

"You're a good man, old friend," he said.

"Let's go," Frank said.

The group got up, and walked out of the conference room.

"Bye, Doc," Charlie said. "Thanks for everything."

"See you soon," he said. "I want to take a look at Hilda before you guys fly the coop."

Charlie nodded.

The caravan back to the RV Park was uneventful. They got to the gate, with the squad car in front. Charlie tooted the horn, and Hilda came out. She opened the gate, and the squad car rolled in, followed by the SUV. They pulled both vehicles back behind the clubhouse, and the dispersed.

"Let's go to the clubhouse before we go back to the rig," Jane said. "I want to be there if Hilda needs us. This is going to be hard for her."

Frank nodded, and they walked over in that direction. They came in through the door just as Charlie and Hilda got together. Hilda threw her arms around Charlie. She was happy to see him, but then got a concerned look on her face when Charlie started to cry.

"What's the matter?" she asked, pulling back and looking him in the face.

"We lost Chester, Hilda," he said.

"Oh, no," Hilda said. She started crying too, and the held each other for a few moments.

Frank and Jane watched silently, fighting back their tears.

"How about the Sheriff and the Deputy?" she asked.

"They're both going to make it," Charlie said. He smiled through his tears. "Doc said that the Sheriff was already flirting with the nurses."

"Oh, thank God," Hilda said. "What else happened? How did Chester die?"

"I'll go over all of that with you, but I want to get you thinking about something."

"What?" she asked. There was a concerned look on her face.

"The General sat us down and talked to us when we were over at the hospital. He wants to move us somewhere else."

"Everybody?" Hilda asked.

"No, just the core group of people," Charley said. "Jeb, Earl, Frank, Jane, Jerry, Jasmine, Jackson, and me."

"You're leaving?" Hilda said. She started crying again.

"I'm not going anywhere without you," he said. "I want you to leave with me."

"What about the park?" she asked.

"The Army would like to stay here," Charlie said. "Make this their base of operations. You would be able to come back after this is over."

"So what are they going to do? Protect a caravan of RVs?"

"No, their proposal is to fly us out with as much stuff as we can carry, and we'll be provided with new RVs courtesy of Uncle Sam at our destination."

"Are you alright with that?" asked Hilda.

"I don't want to give up my rig," Charlie said. "It's only a couple of years old, but we can have them back if they survive the war."

Hilda thought for a few minutes. Then she looked back at Charlie.

"So you want me to tear off into the sunset with you," she asked. "I'll do it, but I have one condition."

"What's that?" he asked.

"Marry me," she said. She had a scared look on her face as she watched for his reaction.

Charlie started laughing.

"Sweetie, I was going to ask you anyway," Charlie said. "Couldn't you tell?" He pulled her over to him and kissed her. When they broke the kiss, she looked up at him.

"Yes," she whispered.

"Well, we'd better make this official," Charlie said. He got down on one knee and took her hand.

"Will you marry me, Hilda?" he asked.

"Yes, Charlie," she said. "Now get up here before you get stuck down there."

They got up and hugged again. Frank and Jane clapped, and they turned around, embarrassed.

"I forgot you two were in here," Charlie said.

"There a preacher around here?" asked Frank, grinning.

"I know one, and we need him here anyway," Charlie said. "For Chester's memorial."

Frank nodded. He looked down at Jane.

"Should we go back to our rig and leave these two love birds alone?"

"Yes," Jane said. They walked out the door and headed to their space.

"We have a lot to do," Frank said as they walked.

"Packing up?" she asked.

"Well, yes, and winterizing the coach. It freezes here."

"Oh, yeah," she said. "You know how?"

"Yes, I've read about it. Doesn't sound too hard."

"Wonder how Mr. Wonderful is going to enjoy the flight?" Jane asked, smirking.

"We might want to put in earplugs, because he's going to yowl. I'm sure Lucy will be alright with it, though."

As they approached the rig, Lucy started to bark. Frank unlocked the door and opened it. She bounded out, jumping up at both of them and wagging her tail furiously. Frank and Jane climbed up into the rig, and Lucy followed them.

"I'd better take her out for a quick walk," Frank said.

"Alright, go ahead. I'll make us something to eat."

"Walk?" Frank said to Lucy, as he picked up her leash. She jumped up and down with excitement. Frank hooked her up and grabbed the poop bags. They went out.

Lucy went from place to place, sniffing and doing her business. Frank looked out over the park. What would happen to the folks who weren't part of the core group?" Would they stay? Would General Walker agree to relocate them too if they wanted to leave? There were about another twenty rigs there, over and above the core group. Frank saw Jerry get out of his rig. He walked over.

"What do you think?" Jerry asked, as he joined them walking down the road.

"We haven't finished discussing it yet, but I'm pretty sure we'll be going."

"Us too," Jerry said. "Hate to leave the rig behind. I still owe a lot of money on it."

"How did Rosie take the news about Chester?"

"Hard," Jerry said. "That's why I left the rig. When that old girl starts crying it makes me cry too, and I've done enough of that lately."

"Wonder if Charlie is going to convince Hilda to go? She's pretty strong willed."

"She already agreed," Frank said. He laughed.

"What?"

"She told Charlie she would go with him if he married her."

Jerry stopped in his tracks and started cracking up.

"I should have seen that one coming," he said. "How did he react?"

"He said he was going to ask her anyway, and then he got down on one knee and did a formal proposal. It was quite touching, actually."

"Great," Jerry said. "What about all these folks who weren't part of the core group?"

"That's what I was thinking about when you walked over. I don't know. I wonder if the heat will really be off if word gets around that we are gone."

"Some of the cretins may assume that their supplies are still here."

"Maybe the Army will make as big a deal about using this as a base as they do about us leaving," Frank said.

Jerry nodded. "There is one thing that worries me, though," he said.

"What's that?"

"You know damn well that we've had a lot of leakage of enemy personnel into areas that we consider 'safe' now."

"Yes, you are probably right about that."

"So if they are in contact with the militia here, they may still try to hunt us down, and we will be in a strange place without the support system we have built up here."

"That has crossed my mind," Frank said. "I think we'll need to keep moving, and hide our whereabouts as best we can."

"Yes."

"Well, I'd better get back. Jane is making us something to eat, and I'm really hungry."

"Okay. I assume we'll see you two in the clubhouse later?" Jerry asked.

"Yes, the General is coming over, and I'd like to chat some more with him and Major Hobbs too. We also have a wedding and a funeral to plan."

Jerry nodded, and walked back to his rig.

Frank opened the door of the rig and got in, with Lucy bounding ahead of him. Jane already had food down in their bowls, and Mr. Wonderful was attacking his. Lucy ran over to hers and started eating too. Jane was in the bedroom. Frank could hear her talking to somebody.

"That's great honey," she said. "I'll worry about you, but I think you're doing the right thing." Jane looked up and saw Frank walking into the bedroom. "Here's your father. Want to say hello?"

Frank nodded and sat down on the bed next to Jane.

"Alright, Robbie, love you too. Here's your father." She handed the phone to Frank.

"Hi, son, how are you doing?" Frank asked.

"Good, dad. We're getting ready to leave…..a couple of days. I'll lock everything down in the condo before we take off."

"Thanks, son. You're mother told you that we are leaving Utah, correct?"

"Yes, she did. I think that's good. You aren't in a good place."

"We were hoping we could come back to California, but they are sending us east."

"You don't want to come back here, dad."

"Really? Why not."

"This isn't free anymore," Robbie said. "We're still under martial law. There is some scary stuff going on."

"Scary?"

"Yes. Won't say any more on the phone."

"Why did you enlist?"

"To get into the fight against the bad guys."

"You aren't making sense."

"I'll fill you in later, dad."

"Alright. Heard from Sarah?"

"She hasn't called you yet?" Robbie asked. He snickered. "Chicken."

"What?"

"Just call her dad. She's good, don't worry. She has something to tell you."

"Hmmm," Frank said. "Alright, we'll call her. Love you son, take care."

"You take care too, dad. Love you."

Frank put down the phone and looked at Jane.

"That was a strange phone call," he said. "Did he say anything to you about California?"

"No, why?"

"He said not to come back there. He said it's bad."

"Oh," she said. "That's strange. He told me he enlisted. I think he was afraid to talk to me about it."

"Did he say anything to you about Sarah?"

"No, he didn't," she said. "But I heard you asking him. What's up?"

"I think we'd better call her right now," Frank said. He dialed the number. It rang several times, and then there was a click.

"Mom?" Sarah asked.

"No, it's dad," Frank said. "I'm on mom's phone. Everything alright, honey?"

"Is mom there with you," she asked.

"Yes, she's right next to me." Frank said.

"Good. Would you put the phone on speaker? I have something to tell both of you."

Frank looked over at Jane, and then put the phone on speaker.

{ 11 }

Capitol Crime

Frank and Jane stared at the phone, waiting for their daughter to speak.

"Mom, dad, can you both hear me now?" asked Sarah. She sounded nervous.

"Yes, sweetheart, we've got you on speaker," Frank said. "What's up?"

"I'm married," she said. Frank and Jane looked at each other.

"Who did you marry?" Jane asked.

"Steve. He's my roommate's cousin. You know, the one that I was staying with in Boise."

"Is he a good man?" Frank asked. "Does he have a career?"

"Yes, Daddy," she said. "He's an EMT, and is working towards getting a job as a fireman in Boise."

"You're still in Boise?" Jane said.

"Yes, I won't be going back to Portland. I found a job here already."

Frank and Jane looked at each other and smiled.

"Well, congratulations, sweetheart," Frank said. "I wish we could come right over and see you, but there isn't a way to get there right now. In fact, they are moving us further east soon."

"Who's they?" asked Sarah.

"The Army. Long story……I can't tell you everything now. We're really glad you stayed in Boise. This General that we met yesterday told us it is safer than Portland. That's why we were calling you… we were hoping you were still there, and were going to suggest that you stay."

"Oh," Sarah said. "That sounds kinda scary, you being moved by the Army."

"Don't worry, honey," Jane said. "We'll be fine. Maybe you could sent pictures of the wedding, if you have any."

"It was just at the court house, but I do have some pictures of the two of us. I'll e-mail them to you."

"Perfect," Frank said. "You didn't have to be afraid to tell us this, you know. We just want you to be happy, and we know you're a good judge of character."

"Yes," Jane said. "As long as you two love each other, you'll be fine."

"I love him so much, mom," Sarah said. She started to choke up.

"Good," Frank said. "We're so happy for you, sweetie."

There was a tap on their door. Frank got up and walked over. He saw Jerry standing outside. He opened the door.

"The General is in the clubhouse," Jerry said. "We're going over in a few minutes."

"Great, we'll be there soon." Frank shut the door and went back into the bedroom.

"That was Jerry. The General is in the clubhouse."

"Great," Jane said. "Sarah, we have to go now. There's a meeting starting up. Thanks so much for telling us. I love you, sweetie. Stay safe."

"I love you too, Sarah," Frank said. "Take good care of your husband. We'll talk to you soon."

"Love you guys," Sarah said. "Bye."

She hung up. Jane picked up her phone and looked up at Frank.

Bug Out! Part 4 – Mortars and Motorhomes

"You okay with this?" she asked.

"Yes, as long as he treats her right. Firemen usually want to take care of people, so that's a good thing. I'm so relieved that she's staying in Boise."

"Me too. Ready to go?" she asked.

"Sure," Frank said. They both got up and walked into the salon. Lucy was jumping up and down.

"Should we take her?" asked Jane.

"Sure, why not," Frank said. "She'll be good. Come here girl, let's get your leash on."

Lucy scampered over and stood still as Frank attached the leash. He grabbed the poop bags on the way to the door.

"See you later, Mr. Wonderful," Frank said, looking at the cat. He was sitting on the dashboard looking out the window, but he casually shot a glance to Frank and Jane as they opened the door and stepped out. Frank locked it up, and they started towards the Clubhouse.

"Before the world went crazy, I would have been upset that Sarah up and got married without saying anything to us. I'm glad now," Jane said. "I'm going to miss being involved in a wedding for her, though." Her eyes were glassy. Frank pulled her close as they walked.

"I know, sweetie. I'm sorry about that," he said.

They got to the clubhouse just as Earl and Jackson were walking up.

"Hey, guys," Frank said, smiling at them. They both smiled and nodded. Inside were Charlie and Hilda, General Walker and Major Hobbs, Jerry and Jeb.

"Where's Jasmine and Rosie?" Jane.

"They'll be along in a few minutes. Rosie had to primp a little bit before meeting the General." He grinned. Jane and Frank cracked up.

"Well, at least this will take her mind off of Chester for a little while," Jane said.

They walked over to where the General and Major Hobbs were talking with Hilda and Charlie.

"Frank, how are you," Major Hobbs said. "And Jane. I heard that you and Jasmine saved the day."

"And Chester," Jane said.

"So sorry to hear about what happened to him," Major Hobbs said. "He was a good man."

"Yes, he was," Frank said. "You know he's the person who told us about Charlie's place, and that's how we ended up here."

"That's right," Charlie said. "I had a gun on you folks until I saw that Chester was with you."

"You have an RV Park too?" asked General Walker.

"Yes, but it's near the Grand Canyon," he said. "I had to leave it."

"Oh, I assumed that this place was yours and Hilda's," General Walker said.

"Well, it will be soon enough," Hilda said, smiling. "We're getting married."

"Ah, great news," General Walker said. "I was very impressed with Charlie while we were in town. Good man."

"Yes he is," Hilda said. Charlie looked embarrassed.

"Where new General?"

It was Rosie and Jasmine, walking through the door. Everybody turned and smiled at them as they walked up. The General gave Major Hobbs a quizzical look, and Hobbs cracked up.

"Rosie – she's Jasmine's mother, and she's quite a card," Major Hobbs said. "How much you want to bet she asks you if you're married."

"I don't think I'll take that bet, Major, judging by the faces in the crowd here."

"Oh, handsome General," Rosie said as she looked him over. "You married?"

Everybody cracked up.

"Yes, I am," he said.

"Too bad," she said.

"Not saying anything?" Frank asked Jasmine. She rolled her eyes.

"Did you ever see it do any good?" she said, smirking.

"How about Happy Hour?" Rosie asked.

"Well, I guess we could have some cocktails," Hilda said. "I think we deserve it."

"Oh, and congrats on engagement, Hilda. You got good man," Rosie said.

"Thank you, dear," Hilda said. "Charlie, want to help me get out the cocktail cart? I'm still not 100%."

"Of course, lead the way," Charlie said. They walked off towards the kitchen area.

"Well, you still available," Rosie said to Jeb. He turned red.

"I don't think I could handle you, Rosie." He snickered. "Might be fun to try, though."

"Alright, you two," Jasmine said. Jerry was standing next to her cracking up.

"I don't know, I couldn't think of a better father in law to have than Jeb," he said.

"Now you talkin'," Rosie said.

"General, we have a question," Frank said. "There are about twenty more rigs that came here with us. They haven't been directly involved in the fighting, but they've been helping out in other ways. If they want to stay with us, can Uncle Sam accommodate that?"

"Major Hobbs told me about that. I've got a question in about that to folks at the Pentagon. Do you have any idea how many of them would like to go?"

"No, I really don't," Frank said. "Possibly none. There are some down sides to going beyond losing our rigs."

"What do you see as the other downsides?" asked the General.

"I can take this one," Jerry said. "I'm thinking that at least some of the enemy have already leaked out to the east."

"Good assumption," the General said.

"If they are in contact with the militia here, we are liable to have enemy folks coming after us, even if we are a couple of states to the east. We won't have the infrastructure and support there that we have here."

"That's a valid concern," the General said. "You have to weigh the risks of that against the risks of staying here."

"We get to take all of our weapons with us, correct?" asked Jeb.

"Well, everything but the tank," Major Hobbs said, laughing. Jeb cracked a smile.

"Who wants a drink?" asked Charlie, as he and Hilda rolled the cocktail cart over.

"Wow, this nice," Rosie said. "You didn't use before."

"No, we just used the tables by the stage last time," she said. "But it's too much work to get all of that set up now."

"I make Weng Weng for anybody who wants," Rosie said. She got next to the cart.

"Beware of those things, gentlemen," Frank said to the Major and General. "They will peel paint off a barn."

"We aren't going to be drinking," General Walker said. "Too much enemy activity."

"Well, I'll have something," Jeb said. "Just whiskey, though." He picked up a short glass off of the tray, used the tongs to put a couple of ice cubes in, and then filled the glass with Jack Daniels. He swirled the glass and backed away, taking a sip. "Oh, yeah."

"There is one thing we would like you guys to do before you leave," Major Hobbs said.

"The security cameras?" asked Frank.

"You got it."

"No problem," Frank said. "We can probably finish all of the installations tomorrow. It might take me another day to get the software set up."

"We won't be able to get you out of here for at least four days anyway," General Walker said.

"Where are you proposing we get dropped off?" asked Charlie.

"We were going to suggest a place outside of Oklahoma City," he said.

"Okla-by God-homa," Jeb said, raising his glass. Everybody looked over at him. "Used to work with an old Okie named DC Winters. That's what he called it. He came west during the dust bowl."

"Of course you guys don't have to stay there.....you have most of the Midwest and South to choose from."

"I think we will need to keep moving," Jerry said. "Just in case the bad guys are still looking for us."

"I would advise that," Major Hobbs said. "And keep your eyes open at all times."

"This doesn't sound very safe," Jane said.

"Well, again, like I said, you have to weigh the safety of that versus the safety of staying here," General Walker said. "As of right now, I believe it's a lot safer to leave."

"How about the replacement rigs?" asked Charlie. "Anything more about them?"

"Yes, actually," the General said. "Apparently we've been supplying a lot of these to people who we've been relocating. We have contracts with several of the large manufacturers. They will get as close to the model that you have now as they can."

"What manufacturers?" asked Jerry.

"Fleetwood, Forest River, Thor, and Winnebago," he said. "If you had an expensive one, you can trade it across, but the deal is a little different than I thought. If you take the basic model, which is an entry level Thor, you can use it until this is over, then give it back and get your old rig back."

"Assuming your old rig is still in one piece," Jeb said.

"Yes, but you will be compensated if it's not. If you want a match to a more expensive coach, Uncle Sam will keep your rig, and probably re-deploy it to somebody else eventually. We might even use it here, if Central Command feels that they want to put a lot more troops in here."

Hilda got a worried look on her face.

"I am going to get my park back when this is over, correct?" she asked.

"Oh, yes, of course," General Walker said. "And we'd take good care of it. If it gets damaged, we'll fix it."

Jane looked at Frank and smiled.

"We should be able to get another Georgetown 328. I know Forest River is still making them," she said.

"Yes, that suits me fine," Frank said. "Not looking forward to the new rig shakedown, though."

"Here, Jackson," Rosie said, handing a Weng Weng to him. He took a sip and his eyes lit up.

"Damn, this is tasty, and it goes down easy too," he said.

"Did you watch her mix that, Jackson?" asked Jerry, laughing.

"No, why?"

"Its way stronger than it tastes," he said. "Think Zombie, or Long Island Iced Tea."

"Oh," he said sheepishly.

"Be man, you can handle," Rosie said. She grinned.

"Now mom, don't try to get everybody plastered," Jasmine said.

"They big boys now," she said. Then she smirked, and took a big slug of her own Weng Weng.

"She's certainly the life of the party, isn't she," General Walker said, grinning.

Bug Out! Part 4 – Mortars and Motorhomes

"You don't know the half of it," Jerry said.

The door opened. Everybody turned and saw the Sheriff hobble in slowly. Lucy barked, and wagged her tail. When the Sheriff got close, she jumped up and sniffed his leg. The Sheriff bent down and petted her head.

"Hi, everybody," he said. "What's cookin?"

"Sheriff, so glad to see you up and around," Frank said.

"Want drink?" Rosie said.

"Sure, but no Weng Weng. I learned my lesson with those," he said. "You'll take advantage of me." He chuckled.

"We heard you were giving those nurses a run for their money," Jane said.

"Oh, yeah, I love to flirt with nurses," the Sheriff said with a grin. "Too bad I didn't need any sponge baths."

"I give if you want," Rosie said. "I nurse."

Everybody in the room cracked up, and Jasmine rolled her eyes again, then shook her head.

"Seriously, folks, I just wanted to thank you for saving me. You didn't have to do that."

"Oh yes we did, you old coot," Jeb said. "You'd have done the same for any of us."

"Yes, I would," he said. "And thanks for saving my nephew, too. He's the last family I have left."

"We are going to be moved out of here, Sheriff," Charlie said. "Maybe you could come with us. You've probably got a target on your back too."

"I figured, that's why I wanted to get over here. To make sure I thanked all of you," he said. His eyes started to mist up. "I can't leave, though. I'm the only law enforcement that we have in the town. I don't even have any deputies to hand it off to."

"Sheriff, I was going to offer the same deal to you," General Walker said. "You are probably being used as a propaganda target too. Your town would be safer if you and your deputy hit the road."

"We could use you, Sheriff," Charlie said. "It might get rough out there."

"But what about the town?" he asked.

"Don't worry about that, Sheriff," General Walker said. "We'll be bringing more folks in here. We could always station a detachment in your Sheriff's station and have them patrolling."

"Can they be nice?" the Sheriff asked. "This is a town full of civilians…mostly older folks but also a bunch of rednecks who live on the outskirts. Those rednecks can be independent and stubborn as hell. I don't want to see them getting shot by some private."

"We'd put good people in there, Sheriff," Major Hobbs said. "But I understand how you feel. Think it over. We've got a good three days before we need a decision."

"Fair enough," the Sheriff said. "I've got to talk it over with my nephew as well. I also need to find out when he's coming out of the hospital. I doubt he'll be out in four days. He got pretty messed up."

"Don't worry, we'll airlift him out when the time comes," General Walker said. "Do you have an RV?"

"Yes, I've got a nice Monaco Camelot sitting in my backyard."

"Well, we could give you an approximate replacement, new, from a handful of manufacturers, but you'd need to bring your rig in here and park it, so Uncle Sam can take it over."

"Oh, you guys aren't driving out of here?"

"No, way too dangerous," General Walker said. "The plan right now is to airlift you with as much as you can carry to a location right outside of Oklahoma City. You'll pick up your new rigs there, and then be free to go where you want to."

"Alright, makes sense," the Sheriff said. "I'll think on it. Is there going to be a memorial for Chester?"

"Yes, we are going to have that here, tomorrow afternoon," Hilda said. "The Reverend will be here. The body won't be brought over, though…..he wanted to be cremated, so the mortuary in town is taking care of that."

"Alright, I'll be here of course."

"And you have to stay after the wake," Hilda said. "There's going to be a wedding."

"Really?" Who's getting hitched?"

"Charlie and I," Hilda said. The Sheriff's face lit up.

"She finally hog tied you, did she?" the Sheriff said to Charlie. "I saw that coming."

"Yes, she's got me hog tied alright, but I'm glad," Charlie said. The two men shook hands, and then hugged.

"I know you'll take good care of her," Sheriff said. "And I know she'll take good care of you."

Frank looked over at Jerry and Charlie, and nodded at them to join him over in the corner. They followed him away from the main group.

"Want to get going early on the security system tomorrow morning?" asked Frank.

"Suits me, Frank," Charlie said.

"Me too," Jerry said.

"Good. I'm hoping we can get the physical installation done by the end of the day tomorrow. I'll work the software too, but I probably won't get it done until the following day. It's a fairly complex job."

"Any chance you can set this up so Hilda can monitor her park remotely when we're gone?"

"Of course," Frank said. "It's going to be on the internet. Security is the thing that's going to take the longest. We don't want the enemy being able to hack in and use the cameras against us. Once I've got that set up, we'll all be able to access the whole system from wherever we are."

"That's great news," Charlie said.

"Hey!" shouted Earl. He had his iPHONE in his hand, and was looking at the screen. "Turn on the TV. Something bad has just happened in D.C."

"Uh oh," Hilda said. She picked up the remote and switched the TV on. There was an image of the smoking wreckage of the U.S. Capitol building.

"Oh, no!" General Walker said. "There was a joint session of Congress going on today. All of our legislators were there."

To be continued in Bug Out! Part 5

ABOUT THE AUTHOR

Robert G Boren is a writer from the South Bay section of Southern California. He writes Short Stories, Novels, and Serialized Fiction.

Made in the USA
Lexington, KY
01 August 2018